New Italian Women

236

New Italian Women

A Collection of Short Fiction

EDITED BY

MARTHA KING

ITALICA PRESS
NEW YORK
1989

ITALICA PRESS, INC.

595 Main Street
New York, New York 10044

Library of Congress Cataloging-in-Publication Data

New Italian women: a collection of short fiction / edited by
Martha King.
        p.   cm.
    Translated from the Italian.
    ISBN 0-934977-16-X : $14.95
    1. Italian fiction -- Women authors -- Translations into
English. 2. Italian fiction -- 20th century -- Translations into
English. 3. English fiction -- Translations from Italian. I. King,
Martha. 1928-
PQ4253.A9N49 1989
853'.01089287'0904 -- dc20   89-45539

Printed in the United States of America
5 4 3

Cover Photo: James Stokoe
Cover Design: Nora Crain

This translation has been made possible
in part through a grant from the
Wheatland Foundation, New York.

1000859880

CREDITS

CONTENTS

Contents

INTRODUCTION

After many years of neglect, women writers in Italy are beginning to receive the attention they deserve. They are not only recipients of coveted annual literary prizes but are taking first place on the vaunted bestseller lists. This attention has been long overdue as Italian women have been writing professionally for more than a hundred years. A number of talented and ambitious women ventured into print in the latter nineteenth and early twentieth centuries in conjunction with the upsurge of feminism and the interest in socialism and universal education. At the same time the proliferation of women's magazines opened up a new forum for their efforts, as did the field of journalism. While most of the magazines designed for women provided their readers with escapist sentimental romances, Sibilla Aleramo, Ada Negri, Matilde Serao and others were exploring – realistically, lyrically, critically – the traditional roles of women in their fiction and enacting these new roles in their own lives. And Grazia Deledda, isolated and unschooled, was teaching herself to walk the narrow line between realism and melodrama in her poignant tales of a disappearing Sardinia. For her fiction she was the first Italian woman to be awarded the Nobel Prize for literature, in 1926.

This initial impetus was soon to flag. Two World Wars and the era of Fascism relegated most Italian women to the traditional concerns of home-keeping and child-raising. Only a few women dared – or were allowed the opportunity – to speak, such as Deledda, and later Natalia Ginzburg.

Women's fiction had a second burst of activity after the second World War with writers such as Elsa Morante, Anna Banti, Alba De Crespedes, Dacia Maraini, and Anna Maria Ortese who developed and expanded the body of women's literature begun in the previous century. Although these women were writing well, and not only on subjects of interest to women, it was still a relatively small and for a long time a generally neglected group.

After nearly a century of change in attitudes and expectations, and years of hard-won professional and creative growth, there is an impressive number of women writing fiction in Italy in the late 1980s. For this change in the political and social condition of women, they are wittingly or unwittingly indebted to the efforts of the women's liberation movement in collaboration with the Italian Communist Party. (Anna Banti disclaimed any interest in group advocacies, while Dacia Maraini and Maria Occhipinti have joined with the struggle for a variety of social reforms.)

Though many of these women writers have only recently received critical acclaim, most of them have been writing and publishing for many years. Anna Maria Ortese, whose *L'Iguana* has been called one of the best books of the past ten years, published her first novel in 1937; Paola Drigo was not well-known until her novel *Maria Zef*, published in 1936, was made into a TV film in 1981. Rosetta Loy's first little-noted novel appeared in 1974, but in 1988 her *Le strade di polvere* was not only a bestseller but it won two literary prizes.

The works making up this anthology have not been chosen from the worthy works of the pioneers, those few self-aware, ambitious and heroic women writers of the nineteenth and early twentieth centuries, but are by the mature writers of the '80s who have built upon the efforts of their precursors. The one exception to the rule governing selection is the inclusion of Grazia Deledda's short story – an inclusion justified by the renewal of interest in her in the United States.

For many years only the names of Morante and Ginzburg were readily recognizable in the United States and England. Now, thanks to a resurgence of translations, Ortese, Banti, Maraini, Morandini, Drigo and others are winning a growing audience. It is hoped that this volume will augment the international appreciation these women deserve.

The subjects treated by women writers have expanded as women's horizons have broadened; attitudes have changed in concert with changes taking place in personal lives, the family, work-place, and society at large. However, the fact remains that these women tend to recreate their environment in close detail – a tendency seen from the earliest novels of Matilde Serao. Such care in observation of rooms, furniture, knickknacks, houses, gardens, does unite the women authors gathered here. Even Dacia Maraini, whose story is largely set in a factory, carefully pictures the rooms where her characters live and the food they eat – not as background or props for the drama, but as essential elements of plot.

But subject matter is not confined exclusively (if it ever was) to the typically traditional occupations of women, such as house and family relationships. Francesca Sanvitale details the deterioration of a male novelist; Marina Mizzau presents vignettes where her characters act out small, touching dramas in a variety of settings, and Dacia Maraini ventures on the previously forbidden ground of love between two women.

The women in this collection deal not only with the concerns of their time, but in many cases their fiction is significantly colored by their specific region. This is characteristic of the fiction of a country that is made up of greatly diverse areas – even though television is slowly eroding sharp contrasts. Fabrizia Ramondino is Neapolitan, and the essence of her work is nourished by that southern culture. Gina Lagorio often recreates scenes of the Ligurian coast in her fiction. Paola Drigo's inventions are steeped in northern Italy, and Sicilian life and customs unmistakably flavor the work of Maria Occhipinti.

Though from different regions and writing out of disparate experience, these women have several notable characteristics in common. They write with an ease born of confidence in their art, and they exhibit a control, an apparent emotional detachment, that allows a deeply ironical view of their invented world to play below the surface. Another distinctive by-product of this apparent ease and control is a succinctness, a skill in limiting details that reveals more than layers of detail possibly could. These women also share a talent for contriving psychological insights that continually surprise and touch the reader. Such resemblances do not suggest imitation or fashion; they are simply the traits of fine writing.

One Italian critic has said that fiction is either metaphorical or autobiographical and private (letters, diaries), but that the best writing combines the two. Such a combination of creative stimuli marks the writing here. Many of the stories are based on personal recollection, rather than pure invention, but issue from a maturity of style that permits memory to be cast in metaphorical form.

The reader will note that many of these works are excerpts from novels. This form was dictated by the reality of Italian reading preferences of the past few decades; that is, the general lack of interest in short stories. Out of necessity the fiction writer was confined to the novel form. Exceptions to this are the short story collections of Dacia Maraini and Anna Banti. This phenomenon is beginning to change. Just as is occurring in the United States, Italian readers are becoming once again more receptive to shorter fiction.

There is a notable inclination among some, such as Monica Sarsini, Marina Mizzau and Milena Milani, to write unusually short pieces, often a mere page or two. The brevity and compactness of these stories makes them the very antithesis of rhetoric (the traditional Italian style); the terseness of these works, dense with subtle meaning and ambiguity, gives them their power and points to a new creative way of expression entirely these women's own.

This collection of fiction by Italian women of the latter half of the twentieth century celebrates a high level of accomplishment. The selections presented here not only continue the tradition of women's literature begun over a century ago, but they inaugurate an exciting vitality in Italian letters that promises continued growth.

Martha King

THE COURAGE OF WOMEN
by
Anna Banti

The group came straggling down by a short cut that threads across the crest of the hill. They were in such a hurry that the upturned rocks rolling down and striking the feet of the three women didn't even amuse the children. The early evening crickets began calling to each other; some dried olives in the fields beyond the walls clattered down from the branches onto the stubble.

No one was chattering or singing anymore as they had an hour ago under the chestnut trees. Only the two little girls, more heedless, still kept their arms around each other and whispered in each other's ears. Then when the silence of the countryside grew deeper, almost nocturnal, and the noise of all those footsteps seemed blindly mechanical, the shortest and palest woman pushed aside the eternal frayed strand of hair that hung to her mouth, and began her litany: "My God, let's hope he's not already home...."

Looking upward, almost imploring the end of the path, she repeated the words softly two or three times with weary sighs. Then her friend on the right, a tall, good-looking woman in tight-fitting clothes, turned to her and almost stopped. Words were certainly her vocation.

1

"Think, silly. What can happen by being a little late? I know the doctor; you have to approach him in the right way. I'll have a few little words with him...."

The conversation was cut off by breathlessness, because the speaker had to run if she wanted to keep up with her companions who were more intent on hurrying than in listening to her counsel. Panting, she managed to reach the lead, leaving behind the friend who had been silent up to now – light-footed, but moving along as if perplexed and absorbed, certainly the least communicative of the three women.

Now the low dry-walls bordering the fields on both sides rose higher, becoming proper walls, and the path became a road. And when they were a few yards from the sharp turn that revealed the first chimneys of the town, smoking at the dinner hour, the short, pale woman stopped. It was the act of an instant, more an inward than an outward expression, but the children also noticed it.

"I won't do it, I won't do it; I'm afraid," the woman moaned in a very quiet voice, head down; she resembled a goat or a countrywoman giving birth. Her two companions were on either side, one encouraging her in a forceful tone, taking upon herself the task of supporting and dragging her along before it was necessary, the other only staring at her in pity, with a lost, fearful intensity. The children gathered around in a circle, and their faces had that uncertain apprehension that can break out in frightened eyes, sobs and cries, or can disperse in a second, like a cloud.

"Don't act like that, Amina, think of the children," the tall woman urged, enunciating in the

soothing falsetto tone used to divert children from
a scene they must not remember; but the children,
almost hostile, tightened the circle. Amina
continued to stand motionless, her face in her
hands. Then suddenly, just like a goat, she changed
her mind and charged ahead quickly, almost
impatiently. Now the comforter had difficulty in
following her and showed by her gestures the
intention of stopping her. The silent companion, on
the other hand, had put wings on her feet and went
ahead with an expression half unconscious and half
wild. Still mute, but fervent right up to her
imperceptibly moving lips, one near her could have
heard her murmur under her breath Amina's last
words: "I won't do it, I won't do it," repeated
without emphasis, like a prayer or a class
assignment that had to be learned.

As they grew near their destination, the subdued
children rocked on their feet and stopped to scrape
the crumbling plaster from the side of the house
with their fingernails; then they were already
through the gate and lined up in the kitchen like
hungry donkeys. The three women gathered in a
tight group with ashen Amina in the middle. Only
her friends looked up toward the house to see some
sign at the door or windows that the master of the
house was home; and they were beginning to cheer
up – "Come on, he is still out" – when they saw him
appear at the side of the awful house, still dressed
in his black hat and suit, but with his collar and tie
loosened: a gloomy and agitated untidiness under
that face of a citizen gone wild. By merely looking
at him they could imagine the bitter, dry lips of a
country squire after a day spent in debauchery: too
many cigars, too many bottles and cards and talk

with too bored friends; the saliva sticks under his tongue. With a heat burning under his skin, his blood-shot eyes see everything as unjust, polluted, hostile: his harvest poor, his house in shambles, his children badly brought up and that wife – that wife with cat eyes. "Damn the Maremma where I found her and which has reduced me to this state," he had been thinking all the way home, kicking stones. And now what will he say?

The women have stopped: better to leave to the husband the choice of arms and the initiative of the first outburst. Feverishly Amina tidies her fallen lock of hair and seeks her voice to respond to the first peals of thunder; Rosa is spellbound, but Norma believes in the right moment and takes a chance. With tiny steps such as one makes not on the trodden ground of a courtyard but in a large room among knickknacks, she advances: elbows close to her sides, hands pressed to her stomach. It appears the man cannot see clearly, the scant light of the sunset flees like the thread of his great rage, difficult to change itself as quickly as he would have liked into a whip, a rope, into the most offensive instrument possible. Suddenly he finds under his nose that small body, those round shoulders, and a smiling little mouth. Jokes about the beautiful widow who plays the romantic lady of the manor are all very fine: but in the sunlight, in the morning, when one has a fresh head. Now they seem only enemies – these women! who give support to his daily enemy, and instead of running away confront him with this voice like a frivolous pigeon that charms with song and then double-crosses: "The fault is all mine, doctor! Amina would have come back long ago, but I heard a

nightingale on the plain below and I detained her.
You forgive me, don't you, doctor?"

And her little curved hands flutter like a
butterfly, echoing the little motions of her bowed
head luxuriant with curls, bows and feathers. Many
years ago a small, thin, brilliant young doctor had
adored the apologies of beautiful women; but for
the poor, mean little man who has taken his place
everything is poisoned, and these beautiful manners
seem to him like betrayals. The few remains of his
worldly memories are so disturbing that he suffers
embarrassment for his loosened tie and unshaven
face. His liver hurts, his rage grows; and he
doesn't make her wait for his reply: "I don't give a
damn about you or your feathers!"

The swiftness with which difficult situations and
shameful quarrels between civilized people are
resolved is always a mystery. An instant after the
incredible invective there was no longer anyone in
front of the villa. Without good-byes or apologies
Amina and Rosa disappeared through the door; the
husband vanished and Norma was on her way home
and already in sight of her gate. The crickets
chirped plaintively in the distance: "uncouth, ill-
mannered, alcoholic" railed Norma through tight
lips, slamming the door a little harder than usual.
The "Good evening, Signora" of the gardener
seemed to her like amends for an insult, a
deliberate homage that required recognition with a
rather solemn nod of her head.

Groping their way in the dark up the steep stairs,
Amina and Rosa separated without a word. One
entered the conjugal bedroom and the other the
little room where she was staying during her visit
with her cousin. The beds, curtained with mosquito

netting, seemed like phantoms' snares, silent
stranglers at that dark hour. Once the door was
shut, Rosa couldn't let go of the handle or go
through the steps necessary to remove her clothes
and put on a house dress. She was staring at the
still white space of the window, anxiously noting
the sounds, the voices, the slamming of doors on
the floor below. The children were arguing far
away, perhaps in the kitchen, and their sharp cries
reached her from time to time, muffling every other
sound. The maid must have been setting the table
because a clanking of plates and silverware could
be heard, but the husband and wife gave no sign of
life. To mediate, to calm down, to pray? Or to
shut herself up in the bedroom all evening, all
night? Pale Rosa would gladly hold to this last
alternative – Rosa who at thirty had not yet been
able to imagine how one could decide on marriage.
The handle, released and immediately recovered,
was by now hot, damp, anxious itself, like her hand.
So fragile, this separating door, in the face of
violence! But so able to change a room into a
prison, into a hiding place. And here the romantic
Rosa, a different woman from the one who swooned
at the door, enjoyed the situation for a moment: the
victim, the tyrant, the deep night, the desolate
plain, "Siena made me, the Maremma unmade me":
Dante for the women of 1850.

But in her bedroom Amina was unable to allow
herself the consolation of a romantic parallel. Each
day life pursued her on more miserable terms and
with more bitter rancor. There was no respite for
her except in moments like this, when at a
culminating point, humiliation, fear, shame relaxed
into a colorless indifference. In this condition she

needed nothing, not even a refuge against the extreme violence so often threatening her. Besides, ironically, her refuge was in this room, with this big bed, these double pillows, and this lace bedspread she had made when she was fifteen; but nothing here affects her in the least. Amina has not even locked the door, but has closed it halfway so that a bit of the dark hallway is visible in the mirror on the chest of drawers. Let come who will; and above all, let her husband make up his mind when to settle the account this time, too. Almost calmly she removes her clothes, putting on a roughly-lined flannel that pricks her underarms each autumn. She takes her time, is in no hurry, and when she ties the black silk apron to her waist she feels sleepy – a sleepiness that vanishes the moment when, running her hand over the marble of her dresser, it touches a cigar butt in its ashes. This proof that her husband had been in the bedroom earlier, right where she is now, in front of the window, makes her shiver and brings her back to her constant thoughts. Where had Angelo been? He had the appearance of having drunk too much like he has when he comes back from Castagneto. Now her brain is completely awake and absorbed in its usual work of guessing the mood of the master of the house and improvising a defense. Of the apathy from a short time before there remains only a strange, calm reflection that retains her thoughts, and she is, for example, amazed by the absurdity of calling by name, even mentally, a man who after years of misunderstanding must be as alien to her as a stranger. And so she continues to reason in the manner of a "wife," as though randomly recalling some musical notes she can no longer hear.

Below, the three boys and two little girls doze, waiting for supper, and some roasted chestnuts stolen from the pan fall from their hands. Amina notices it immediately; their hands are still dirty from the chestnuts. She will have to command, shout, box their ears. What bother! This mother of five children has always looked a little fearfully and distractedly at her offspring, like a girl left in charge of brothers and sisters who are too grown up. Even when they were in the cradle, all tears and caprice, they seemed like some strange, noisy, dangerous playthings. Most of all she was afraid of the mischief they could do, for the illnesses they could get and for which she must necessarily suffer, as maternal love was for her a relentless, cruel necessity. Now she looks at them, frowning a little at the thought of what she must say to them, but she doesn't say a word, and goes through the polished hall into the kitchen, where Cesira is mistress, and pokes around the pans with the same frowning air she used with her children; thinking of what she should criticize and correct if she had the will and the courage. "What does one need, after all, to be brave?" prompts the calm reflection of a short while ago. And there, by the little door that opens onto the garden, with that customary oily-smooth manner, is the doctor. This is the moment that had to come. Yet Amina, with the maid's presence as excuse, tries to delay it further by turning her back to the door and seizing the ladle in the boiled potatoes. Her eyes have grown larger, her cheeks darken not from the heat of the flame but by the intensification of their greenish cast. At her neck, in a stink of stale tobacco, her husband whispers to her: "Never mind, Signora Contessa, don't dirty your little hands"; and he goes into the hall. Magically Cesira appears behind him with the steaming soup tureen. How has she hidden from her mistress the fact that the soup is ready. What is left for Amina? To go into the garden stumbling over the tomato stakes; to go out past the wall, to run, to reach the woods, to roam around the plains where there is malaria, but where there is also a cart to take her to the coast: to get on a ship, to return to her native Elba at last. She accomplishes this quickly in her imagination in the space of four seconds, with her eyes still fixed on the potatoes, until the sound of the door closing forces her to follow hastily in the tracks of the maid; so she appears in the dining room with the air of having arranged and then followed a procession. With a great scrapping of chairs the children sit down at the table; an anxious Rosa appears at the door of the stairway with her round eyes open wide, and immediately reassured, she also sits. That she does not speak is nothing new.

Here, then, under the hanging blue glass oil lamp, a typical nineteenth-century supper. Handsome family; but the father with his yellow eyes breathes on his plate and doesn't eat, like a suspicious cow. For ten minutes the square nails of his right hand have been tapping the tablecloth with funereal regularity, and no one dares take notice of it – least of all the mother, sitting a little sideways, who gulps down spoons of soup, twisting her neck like an uninvited but tolerated guest. It could be said that the children were well brought up because they do not talk; if only they did not scrape their spoons so much on the bottom of their bowls. None of them is disturbed by the parents' animosity, all of them are ready with shrieks of fear if something should threaten the steady ill humor they are accustomed to. And it is normal in this household for the husband and wife to glare at each other. Waiting for the roast, Rosa stares at the surviving flies on the wall and still moves her lips, chewing on a phrase from yesterday and a month old conversation at Porto Ferraio. The two older children silently give one another fierce elbow jabs: there'll be a row in the boys' room this evening.

But when the roast is served the father ceases his angry taping and turns his face toward the wine bottle. One glass, two glasses. The key to his silence unlocks with the third, and all of them prick up their ears; they flinch, looking at him furtively. He seems very occupied in shredding his meat, in dividing it into little strips as if for a bird's meal. At the same time his lips emit brief, sententious phrases resembling the style of an astrologist at a fair – ambiguous and cautious. He addresses no one, but speaks as though considering a danger that must be approached cautiously, with cunning. He hints at a viper's nest, at accounts to be settled, at extreme but necessary decisions. Every once in a while conversation resumes: his dinner companions hope for a pause, but then notice that, underground, the flow of words has not ceased.

The children bow their heads, eating slowly and blinking as though expecting a smack. Rosa is sorry she has come down and keeps her eye on the door to the stairs, unable to keep her feet still. Hard, very dry, the food passes down Amina's throat, though she continues to swallow, conveying in this haste the throb of her fear, her anxiety to get it over with. She would like a drink, but does not dare stretch out her hand to pour: as though that gesture might expose her. She feels as though she has a crown of big birds around her head, ready to pounce on her neck and temples, and that her jaw will no longer obey her in the end and will squeeze her face in a vice of cold bone.

Meanwhile the maid goes around changing plates. Driven by hungry curiosity she stays, insisting on serving bread. She won't go into the kitchen until the scene is resolved. It won't take much for the doctor to give himself over to one of those violent moods that fascinate her in such a perverse way: pulling a corner of the tablecloth and spilling food and plates on the floor, or pounding his fist on the table to make everything bounce; overturned bottles, spilt wine, pieces of broken glass and the women's cries.

But tonight Cesira waited in vain and however many serving tasks she invented she didn't manage to see anything. Afterwards, sitting in the kitchen with the door open, she forgot to eat in her attempt to overhear something. The fact is that the moment for scenes had passed and from this very evening the dissension between her employers had to change character. At a certain point it seemed that the diners were constrained to silence and even the father's muttering stopped; yet no one got up.

"Should I cough or not?" Rosa asked herself, who had a great desire to do so, when, terrified, she noticed that her cousin's eyes were fixed upon her. His lids blinked, or rather, they winked, and his mouth twisted into a little smile: "You understand,

Rosina," sounded his quiet voice with almost playful confidence, "that woman must be kept in her place." His tone was so natural that the children, stupefied by the meal and the heavy atmosphere, didn't even understand the words, and believing the situation relaxed, pushed back their chairs to get up. Besides, their father (the recipient of suddenly satisfied and mischievous glances) also made a move to get up and look for his pipe. Then something really different happened: too bad that Cesira couldn't enjoy it from the hallway. Amina moved from her place, pulled the bottle of wine toward her and poured a glass to the brim – she who drank only water. Then, on her feet, with the fixed, bright eyes of a serpent, the corners of her mouth curling with two scornful shadows: "Look, this is how much I fear you," she said, drinking it down.

From that evening the air was more breathable in the Vannini house. The air was bracing, as though deactivated by powerful lightening flashes. From that time Amina began to put on weight and lose her persecuted expression. Now her eyes no longer remained half-closed and her features acquired character from the new position of her chin, held higher, almost obstinate, above a faintly puffy neck. At first the gossip, the story of discord between the couple grew in town: fearful things, pistols under the pillow, physical blows. Questioned about their troubles, both husband and wife confirmed the talk; they even seemed to take pleasure each time in adding to it a hair-raising particular.

"Certainly," said Amina, "he keeps a revolver under the pillow, but he is a coward and will never have the courage to shoot me. But one day or another I'll let go a little powder...."

And the doctor at a hunt: "Lead is good for birds; for certain people it takes a knife." Until these statements became so commonplace that no one paid attention to them anymore – some people even began to smile about them. The question remained: how did Amina, who used to faint with fear, become so bold? Someone would hazard one guess, someone else another, especially Norma who pretended to know the whole story; but everyone remained unsatisfied, as Amina never confided in anyone.

Like a thrifty person jealous of his capital, she kept to herself the delights of a courage still fresh from fear and terror. Her fear after the great rage that had pushed her to defiant words and action! The whole scene is still before her eyes: the shadow beyond the table, the sudden swinging of the lamp, so still until then, and that look of her husband, crushed by surprise. She is still standing and puts the empty glass upon a large sauce stain, while the wine floods her stomach with burning heat. Then the cousin's two sticky kisses and the dampness of her tears. "Sleep with me tonight, don't stay with him." She hears these words only after she is already lying on the conjugal bed, alone and trembling like the flame of the candle burning on the dresser; and she remembers also Rosa's look while whispering, fixed on the door where Angelo disappeared.

"Too late," she thinks, looking at her feet, immobile under the blanket like a dead person's; and mentally trying to execute an escape through the hall into the cousin's bedroom, the thought of meeting her husband coming up the stairs, in the dark, makes her teeth chatter. That for one night he might not come up she did not hope or expect: they were both condemned to this common room, and then he would have to avenge himself. He will come up with a revolver in his hand. Certainly by now he had already taken it from the old chest in the studio and loaded it. The furniture never so black as tonight, the yellow brocade on the rustic walls never so funereal. In order not to see them Amina has closed her eyes and while she thinks of the rosary of granite beads that they will put around her neck when she is dead, she is aware of the door handle turning. Cornered, her throat grows rigid: better to die like this, with her eyes closed, not opening them under any condition. She hears the noise of the door, the cautious steps of the man, she registers his breathing and even the moment he stops to look at her, so supine and composed. The great power of habit: the friction of his jacket on the chair, the clink of the coins on the dresser announcing that he is undressing, like any other evening.

"He'll kill me at close range. What painful blows to the chest." Now her eyes are glued shut, but her ears follow and translate the visual meaning of every sound, while from time to time the air moved by Angelo's gestures crosses the face of the woman like a sinister caress. The actions of undressing continue, and Amina registers them with a strained clarity. And suddenly an unexpected yet breathlessly awaited interruption, a heavy breath, as one who has a delicate and unusual object in his hands, then a dull click, something is opened and closed again, a hard object that the man has placed next to the clock.

"The pistol," flashes Amina's thought picturing the object; but her expression does not change. Meanwhile the pressure of her husband's body sitting on the bed to take off his shoes, causing her to turn a little to the left, offers her, along with the relief of a change of position, a strange comfort, as if coming closer to the man, even such an enemy, brings back a sense of warmth, almost of help. But as soon as he is stretched out heavily on the other side of the bed, he also immobile and awake, all her anxiety returns. Her closed eyelids perceive the light of another candle, her ear beats time to the breath of danger. If only she could grow heavy with sleep; her body tingles with warning terror, for the raising of the covers on the left side, the presence of the other body on the common bed. A slight motion, an extended hand would be enough for the very fragile safety to collapse and the smooth grain of the sheet to host a violent blow.

From this point on, for an entire hour in the glowing candlelight, the man and wife battle, unmoving, quiet, attentive. Amina had not been mistaken – on her husband's dresser the old pistol is reflected in the drinking glass. Coming up the stairs the man had caressed it in his pocket, confusedly anticipating an extraordinary relief. The threat of that black lump tight in his fist – the falls, the shrieks, the flight in nightclothes. More than that, to tell the truth, he did not imagine: he did not get as far as the shot, the smoke, the shout. The conclusion immediately followed: "that witch deserves it," but chewed over without emphasis, even with a veil of hesitation, because the witch had for half an hour assumed an importance a bit too accusatory.

Reaching the second floor he saw a streak of light under the door: "Ah, you are here," and he turns the handle. Inside, the quiet is such that for a moment he believes he is alone; then seeing the profile of that rigid shape against the rosy light he feels a kind of repugnance that extinguishes his hostile intentions. He had expected something else, he didn't know what, but something entirely different. Certainly his wife had never refused him this scene, no, never, even if he couldn't remember now how the quarrels, her dismay, her tiresome tears usually began. There and then he couldn't think of anything better to do than undress, obedient to the suggestion of the place. Undressing and finding the pistol in his pocket, he pulled it out with that slight feeling of unease that the civilian faces when handling a weapon. Only when he was lying down did his normal temperament begin to reassert itself. Who had made him go to bed, without being sleepy and with quite other thoughts than of sleeping? He frowns over at his wife, forcing himself to feel anger. But his anger held in check too long misses its aim, it has almost evaporated, leaving in its place an impatience, almost an uneasiness with that pale shape, which extreme fear makes extraordinarily sullen and austere.

"Now I'll take her by the arm and teach her to playact with me," he urges himself, but without doing anything; yet he does not admit that the mere thought of extending his hand, exactly what Amina is expecting, makes his fingers perspire. It is precisely this vague feeling that all at once suggests:

"Might she be dead?" and which almost causes him to jump up as from a catafalque. To keep himself under control he forces himself to lie still, he too on the alert. With his eyes closed he begins to receive the most minute sounds, the sputtering of the candle, the creaking of wood, and finally, his wife's breathing, light and restrained, but which, in short, fills the whole room. It is obvious the woman is pretending to sleep. This knowledge that should have renewed his anger is accompanied by – who knows why – a flavor of suspicion. In the silence her behavior appears to have a mysterious meaning: the passive, deaf resistance of so many years, the discreet tears, and finally, this evening, the open defiance, reveal a careful preparation that has come to a head.

"She pretends to sleep because she is sure of herself, and has plotted something: iron, chloroform, vitriol. Perhaps the delay has even been planned just to incite me to take action." The man's nature, rather gloomy and upset by the bad humor of the day, striving not to yield odiously to supplications and fear, is thrown into the most fantastic suspicions. By now he is in a defensive position, and Amina will never know that that was the moment when she was in real danger. "This woman needs to be put in her place": and it is no longer the notion of a drunkard, but the obsession of a terrified man, almost of a madman. His temples pound, the man begins to count the beats and promises himself that on the one hundredth he will put out his hand and grab her arm. And then, slowly, seeming close enough to touch, the clock below strikes eleven. Only eleven. Who could hold out until tomorrow? Better to get it over with the man decides, and with an effort of will he frees his numb arm, opens his fingers and up, up, he withdraws them from the weight of the covers. Immediately the air seems too fluid, his arm too light; the elbow he is leaning on slips. It slips so that his thumbnail hits the drinking glass and makes it vibrate like a thin wail. His heart skips a beat. The game he is playing seems too difficult. He turns his head imperceptibly toward his wife. She has not budged – or is he mistaken and her face has moved to the left a few inches? As he watches, her face seems to gather shadows around the mouth, those commas of irony that accompany a boast. As if it meant: "just try to come close and you'll see."

Now it seems to him very important to keep an eye on the ambush, the woman's very slow turning, and to prevent its happening. Staying like that, mouth half open, he suddenly feels a great tiredness and his eyes burn, unfit to keep watch. And in fact, her terrible mouth seems to separate from her face to wander over the pillow and hide under it, twisted like a picklock. "The revolver," it seems to shout and he makes a leap, but falls like a feather in a well that closes over him.

There actually has been a leap and Amina, with all her ideas about dying with her eyes closed, opens them wide and is ready to scream, when, instead of the mouth of the pistol, she encounters her husband's face, more sorrowful than grim, eyes shut, mouth half open. A deep and regular breathing commences, as on a thousand other nights. So her husband is snoring, therefore sleeping. Still incredulous, his wife holds completely still and eagerly absorbs the meaning of this marvelous sight. There is no doubt – the head's abandon, the light swelling of his cheeks at every breath, the process of breathing that chokes and hisses, give the promise of security. The fact seems so miraculous that, receiving it like a blessing, Amina accepts it totally, without reservation. Her rigidity relaxes into the inertia of happy tiredness, her blood flows again. Taking her gaze from the sleeper's face, she turns to the wall with placid reassurance: her brain, disconnected, is left to follow the inflated, wandering thoughts of someone who had won a lottery and greedily nibbles on her own desires. She will make Giannina a new dress, that is certain, and recover the arm chairs with the material from this hateful canopy over the bed. These queer thoughts are the luxury of her contentment. Then, reviewing what had happened, from the anxious return home to the crisis of a moment ago, she dares to linger on the particular of Norma's sharp reply, and suddenly has a strong desire to laugh. Slowly she pulls herself up on the pillow and arranges herself like a convalescent. From there her husband's face looks smaller in the ample folds. Coldly she examines his thinning hair, the lucid skin of his nose, the yellowish cartilage of his ear. Her look turns from his ear on the pillow to the candle flame that is too high at this moment. And there, next to the candlestick, is the black pistol. For a moment the woman does not move since the good feeling of her liberation had made her forget the shape of her fear, that weapon imagined and not seen.

"He really did want to kill me," is her first thought, an absorbing reminder; but her second thought has to be completely different because her eyes are already sparkling with activity. The fear is no longer dreadful, as she must show; her head rings with stinging words and fearless laughter that, along with the basso of that disgusting snoring, make a beautiful song.

Just as ideas form images in a dream, Amina finds herself standing barefoot next to the bed without realizing it. She has not yet decided what to do, but the certainty of a power and a victorious cunning induce her to move alongside the bed, keeping her eyes on the sleeper. Turning the corner, she is drawn by the door, but traitorously: something tells her that beyond it she will again feel the pressing anxiety to escape, the terror of being caught. She resists, and dragging her feet over the rough bricks, she strikes one of her husband's shoes; in order not to fall she grabs at the back of the chair where his clothes have been casually thrown. Now she notices the odor of sweat and tobacco as her fingers touch the folds of his vest and sleeves, still alive and elastic: those secret symbols of all her misery. Then a perverse curiosity urges the woman on in pursuit of the visible traces of those actions she had followed with closed eyes an hour ago. It seems like she is unearthing relics, some abandoned bones, and she is suddenly aware of an uneasiness that is not fear, but an inner craving.

Why deny it? Her right hand has touched the wood of the dresser, has come down precisely on the weapon as if the gesture were premeditated. The weight of the object gives her hand the sensation of sudden swelling, but in the action of picking it up it becomes even more heavy. What fear, what fear, Amina says to herself, but she knows she is lying to herself and that her heart is

beating so fast because a mocking little voice
keeps saying: "What do you need? If he wakes up
you'll shoot...." No, fear is not making Amina
short of breath, but the pistol seems to have
become an enormous load, more than her strength
can bear. Her shoulders droop, then her knees.
Almost in a state of sleep her fingers feel the
texture of the bedside rug where her body has sunk.

There, between two house-slippers, teeth chattering, she gets hold of herself. Her right arm is in
pain, and she notices she is still gripping the pistol
tenaciously. Then, with the help of her other hand,
she loosens her fist and cautiously stretches her
fingers. Above her head the man's breathing rises
and falls without pause and becomes a pledge of
protection along with the knowledge of the floor so
near, of the fringe of the blanket at the foot of the
bed. Certain distant memories of childish games
come pleasurably to mind, and they affirm that this
heavy revolver is as useless as it is heavy: at most
good for a joke. Painfully the woman leans on her
hands and rises to a kneeling position. There she
stops, her eyes on a level with the edge of the bed.
In the candlelight her face is haggard, death-like,
yet the shadow of a smile curls the corners of her
mouth and bestows on her bowed head a look of
innocent obstinacy. Her chin grazes her neck, her
curved forehead touches the covers, and she leans
there almost as a counterweight to the action of her
right hand that slowly lifts the weapon and slips it
under the mattress – right there under the body of
her husband. If the thrust of her arm were not so
deliberate and deep it might pass for the gesture of
one who, after the patient is awake, assures herself
that the sheets are tucked in as they should be.

Then the hand reappears empty. And with a childish persistence the left hand massages it, almost caressing it, with her eyes still closed as in a game. The effort to get to her feet, the steps taken to get back into bed, do not register on her conscious mind.

Sitting on the edge of the bed with the simple prudence of one accustomed to sleeping with someone, Amina looks at her wrist with interest, rubs it, yawns. Before lying down she looks at the candle flame, which is now half consumed. She leans toward it with puffed cheeks and blows it out. The return of the dark completely loosens her facial muscles: merely a sleepy face. Now it seems to her that a wall has risen to divide her side from her husband's and to guarantee it, forever. Here she can stretch her poor legs, find a better position by turning on her right side, relaxed. She is almost asleep, and with the intransigence of sleep, registers the annoyance of that snoring and the faint light behind her back. She grasps the pillow carelessly and pulls it over her head to cover her ears.

Translated by Martha King

The Sardinian Fox
by
Grazia Deledda

The long, warm May days had come back, and Ziu
Tomas again sat as he had the year before – ten
years before – in the open courtyard in front of his
house, which was the last in a bunch of little black
buildings huddled against the gray slope of a
mountain. But in vain spring sent its breath of wild
voluptuousness up there: the decrepit old man,
motionless between his old black dog and his old
yellow cat, seemed as stony and insensible as
everything around him.

Only, at night, the smell of the grass reminded
him of the pastures where he had spent most of his
life; and when the moon rose out of the sea, far off,
as huge and golden as the sun, and the coastal
mountains, black beneath a silver sky, and all the
huge valley and the fantastic semicircle of hills
before and to the right of the horizon were covered
with shimmering veils and areas of light and
shadow, then the old man used to think of childish
things, of Lusbé, the devil who leads damned souls
to the pasture, after they have been changed into
wild boars; and if the moon hid behind a cloud, he
thought seriously of the seven calving cows which
the planet, at that moment going to supper,
devoured calmly in its hiding place.

He almost never spoke; but one evening his granddaughter Zana, when she shook him to tell him it was bedtime, found him so stubbornly silent, erect, and rigid on his stool that she thought he was dead. Frightened, she called Zia Lenarda, her neighbor, and both women succeeded in moving the old man, helping him into the house, where he stretched out on the mat in front of the hearth.

"Zia Lenarda, we have to call a doctor. Grandfather is as cold as a corpse," the girl said, touching the old man.

"Our doctor's gone away. He went to the mainland for two months to study ear diseases, because he says they're all deaf around here when he asks them to pay the rent on his pastures...as if he hadn't bought all that land with the people's money, may justice find him! And now, instead of him, we have that foolish snob of a city doctor, who thinks he's the court physician of the king of Spain. Who knows if he'll come or not?"

"Zia Lenarda, he has to come. He charges twenty lire a visit!" Zana said haughtily.

And the woman went off.

The substitute was living in the regular doctor's house, the only habitable one in the whole village. Surrounded by gardens, with terraces and arbors, with a great courtyard covered with grapevines and wisteria, the house was a comfort even to this substitute, who came from a town that, though small, had all the necessities, vices, murderers, loose women, and gambling houses that the larger cities have.

Zia Lenarda found him reading a yellow-backed book in the dining room, which opened onto the courtyard; no doubt a medical work, she thought, judging by the intensity with which he consumed it, his nearsighted eyes stuck to the page, his white fists supporting his dark, rather soft cheeks, his thick lips parted to show his protruding teeth.

The maid had to call him twice before he noticed the woman's presence. He closed the book sharply and, slack and distracted, followed Zia Lenarda. She didn't dare to speak, and went before him as if to show him the way, leaping, agile and silent, down from rock to rock over the rough lanes, struck by the moon.

Below, in the valley's depth, in front of the woman's darkened window, the doctor looked up and saw the mountains' silver peaks. The pure smell of the valley was mixed with the sheepfold odor that came from the hovels, from the forms of shepherds crouched here and there on the steps before their doors: all was sad and magnificent. But in the courtyard of Ziu Tomas the smell of hay and sage dominated; and in front of the low wall by the embankment, with the huge moon and a star almost scraping her head, the doctor saw a woman's form so slender, especially from the waist down, so shrouded, without outlines, that she gave him the impression of a bust set on a narrow pedestal.

Seeing him, she went back to the kitchen, got a light, and knelt down beside her grandfather's mat, while Zia Lenarda ran into the other room to fetch a painted chair for the doctor.

Then the girl raised her head and looked into his eyes, and he felt a sensation that he would never forget. He thought he had never seen a woman's face more lovely and more enigmatic: a broad forehead covered almost to the eyebrows (one higher than the other) by two bands of black, shiny hair; a narrow, prominent chin; smooth cheekbones that cast a little shadow on her cheeks; and white, straight teeth, which gave the suggestion of cruelty to her proud mouth; while her great black eyes were full of sadness and a deep languor.

Seeing herself examined in this way, Zana lowered her eyes and didn't raise them again; but when her grandfather didn't answer the doctor's questions, she murmured: "He's been deaf for twenty years or more."

"You don't say? Well, at least you might prepare a foot bath for him; his feet are frozen."

"A foot bath? Won't that hurt him?" Zia Lenarda asked, consulting Zana. "He hasn't taken his shoes off for eight months."

"Well, then, are you going to leave him here now?"

"Where else can I put him? He always sleeps here."

The doctor got up, and after he had written out a prescription, he gave it to Zana and looked around him.

The place was black as a cave; he could make out a passage at the back, with a wooden ladder; everything indicated the direst poverty. He looked with pity at Zana, so white and thin that she reminded him of an asphodel blooming at the mouth of a cavern.

"The old man is undernourished," he said hesitantly, "and you are, too, I believe. You'd both need a more plentiful diet. If you can…"

She understood at once. "We can do anything!"

Her expression was so full of scorn that he went away almost intimidated.

Up, from stone to stone, along the sandstone path he went back to his oasis; the moon silvered the arbor, and the wisteria blooms hung like bunches of fantastic grapes whose very perfume was intoxicating. The old maidservant was spinning in the doorway, and with Zana's strange face still before his eyes, he asked: "Do you know Ziu Tomas Acchittu?"

Who didn't know the Acchittu family?

"They're known even in Nuoro, my prize! More than one learned man wants to marry Zana."

"Yes, she's beautiful. I had never seen her before."

"She never goes out. There's no need of that, to be sure. The rose smells sweet even indoors. Foreigners come from everywhere, even from Nuoro, and pass by just to see her."

"What? Has the town crier gone around to announce her beauty?"

"That's not it, my soul! The old man is so rich he doesn't know how much he has. Land as big as all of Spain, and they say he has more than twenty thousand *scudi* in a hole somewhere. Only Zana knows the place. That's why she doesn't want even Don Juacchinu, who's noble but not so rich."

"And may I ask where these riches come from?"

"Where do the things of this world come from? They say the old man (on my life, I can't say yes or no about it, myself) had a hand in more that one bandit raid in the good old days when the dragoons weren't as quick as the *carabinieri* are nowadays. Then, in those days, more that one shepherd came home with one sack full of cheese and the other of gold coins and silver plate...."

The old woman began to relate all this, and it seemed that she drew the stories from her memory like the thread from her distaff; the man listened, in the shadow of the arbor, sprinkled with gold pieces, and now he understood Zana's laugh and her words: "We can do anything!"

The day after the first visit he was back at the house: the old man was sitting on the mat, calmly gumming his barley bread soaked in cold water, the dog on one side of him, the cat on the other. The sun slanted in through the low door, and the May wind bore away the wild, leathery smell of the old man.

"How's it going?"

"Well, as you can see," Zana said, with a hint of scorn in her voice.

"Yes, I can see. How old are you, Ziu Tomas?"

"Yes, I still can," the old man said, showing the few blackened teeth he had left.

"He thought you said *chew*. Grandfather – " Zana said, bending over the old man, showing him her hands with all the fingers sticking out except the right thumb, " – like this, isn't that right?"

"Yes, ninety, may God preserve me."

"Good for you. I hope you live to be a hundred – more than a hundred! And you, Zana, you've stayed here with him, alone?"

She told him how all her relatives were dead, her aunts, uncles, cousins, the old, the children; and she spoke calmly of death as of a simple event without importance; but when the doctor turned to the old man, shouting: "Change your way of living! Cleanliness! Roast meat! Good wine! and make Zana enjoy herself a little, Ziu Tomas."

Then the old man asked: "When's he coming back?"

"Who?"

"Oh," Zana said, "it's just that he's waiting for our regular doctor to come back and cure his ears."

"Wonderful! Our doctor's fame is assured then."

The old man, who went on understanding everything in his own way, touched the sleeve of his torn jacket, which was shiny with grease. "Dirty? It's the custom. People who are well off don't have to make a show of it."

As a matter of fact, the doctor observed that the cleanest people in town were the poor; the rich paid no attention to their clothes, scorning appearances, and also finding it convenient perhaps. Here, one day, was Zia Lenarda, waiting for the doctor in the courtyard, dressed like a servant, though she too was a woman of means, with property and flocks, so rich that in spite of her forty-three years she had married a handsome boy of twenty.

"Good morning, doctor, your honor. I'd like to ask a favor of you. My husband Jacu is off on military service: now it's shearing time and I want him to come home on leave. Your honor doesn't know anyone at the Court?"

"No, unfortunately, my good woman."

"I asked our regular doctor about it. Take care of it, I said, if you pass through Rome. But he always says yes, then he forgets. My Jacu is a handsome boy (I'm not boasting just because I'm his wife) and just as good as honey...with a little pushing he could get everything...."

She made a gesture of pushing with her spindle, but the doctor went off, sighing.

"It's not enough to be handsome and good in this world to get what we want, my dear lady."

And he went back to his oasis, thinking of Zana and of many things in his past. He was thinking that in his youth he had been handsome and good and yet he had got nothing, not love, or wealth, or even pleasure. True, he had not hunted for them; perhaps he had been waiting for them to offer themselves spontaneously; and as he had waited and waited, time had passed into futility. But in the past few years he had been seized sometimes by fits of mad rebellion; he sold his property and went off to search urgently for love, wealth, pleasure. But one day he realized that these cannot be bought, and when his wallet was empty, he went back to his few patients, joked with them good-naturedly, took long, absent-minded walks, and read yellow-backed French novels.

Zia Lenarda, on her side, convinced that good looks can obtain everything, seeing that the doctor went to the Achittus' every day even though the old man was well, turned to Zana.

"You tell him, treasure! Everyone's getting ready for the shearing. What can I do, with everything turned over to the hired hands? The doctor looks at you with eyes as big as doorknobs…. How can he help it, dear heart? If you tell him to ask for Jacu's leave, he can't say no."

But Zana didn't promise; and when, after the tedium of those long days when the warm wind, the empty blue sky, the bright sun created an ineffable sadness, the doctor went at evening to the courtyard of Ziu Tomas, where he sat astride the painted chair in front of the hedge, full of fireflies and stars, she joked with him and asked him what causes certain diseases, how poisons are made, and she spoke calmly of many things, but she didn't ask the favor her neighbor wanted.

Sometimes Zia Lenarda herself, seated on the low wall, spun in the dark and joined in the conversation. This annoyed the doctor, who wanted to be alone with Zana after he had convinced the old man to go to bed early because the night air was bad for the deaf. The older woman spoke of nothing but the shearing.

"If you could just see the celebration, your honor! Nothing is more fun, not even the feast of San Michele and San Constantino. I'd invite you if Jacu came, but without him the feast would be like a funeral for me."

"Well, my good woman, do you want to know the truth? They'd give Jacu leave only if you were ill, and you're as healthy as a goat."

Then she began to complain; she had had so many aches since Jacu left, and now that shearing time approached, she really was suffering mortally. To convince the doctor more readily, she took to her bed. He was touched. He wrote out the certificate and ordered some medicine. Zana waited on her neighbor, poured out the dosage, looking at it in the reddish light of the oil lantern, and murmured: "It's not poison, is it?"

Then she went back to the courtyard, where the doctor was sitting on the painted chair. It was an evening in early June, warm already and scented. Night of love and memories! And the memories came, sweet and bitter, from the doctor's dark tortuous past, as from the dark and tortuous valley came the sweet and bitter odor of the oleander. He drew his chair closer to the low wall where Zana was sitting, and they began their usual conversation. Occasionally a shepherd passed in the lane, without too much surprise at hearing the doctor's voice in the courtyard of Ziu Tomas. By now everybody believed that the doctor was regularly courting Zana, and they were sure that Zana would accept him, otherwise she would have kept him at a distance. But the two of them spoke of matters apparently innocent, of grasses, poisonous plants, medicaments.

"Oleander? No, that isn't poisonous, but hemlock is. Do you know what it looks like?"

"Who doesn't?"

"It's called the sardonic plant. It makes people die laughing...like you!"

"Let go of my wrist, doctor. I don't have the fever like Zia Lenarda."

"I have the fever, Zana."

"Well, take some quinine. Or is that poison, too?"

"Why do you keep talking about poisons tonight? Are you planning to kill somebody? If you are, I'll kill him for you at once...but..."

"But?"

"But..."

He took her wrist again, and she allowed it. It was dark anyway, and nobody could see from the lane.

"Yes, I do want some poison. For the fox."

"What? She comes this close?"

"She certainly does! Let go of me," she added in a whisper, twisting threateningly, but he took her other hand and held her fast, as if she were a thief.

"Give me a kiss, Zana. Just one."

"You can go and kiss a firebrand. Well, all right, if you give me the poison. That fox even comes and steals our newborn lambs...."

When Jacu's application for leave had been mailed off, along with the doctor's certificate, Zia Lenarda recovered and went back to minding her neighbors' business. And without any surprise she realized that the doctor was aflame like a field of stubble. He went back and forth in the lane like a boy, and even twice in a day he visited Ziu Tomas, claiming he would cure the old man's deafness before his colleague came back from the mainland. Zana seemed impassive; often she wouldn't make an appearance, but stayed shut in her room, like a spider in its hole.

On Sundays, the only day she went out – to go to mass – the doctor waited for her in front of the church.

One after another, the women came up the winding lane, stiff in their holiday clothes, their hands folded on their embroidered aprons, or carrying their babies on their arms, in red cloaks marked with a blue cross. When they reached a certain spot they turned toward Mount Nuoro, guarded by a statue of the Redeemer, and blessed themselves. The sun gleamed on the gold of their sashes and illuminated their fine Greek profiles. But the doctor, as if bewitched, looked only at Zana, and the old gossips thought: "The daughter of Tomas Acchittu has given him mandrake to drink...."

One day, among the few men who took part in the women's procession, there was Jacu, home on leave. He was really handsome, no two ways about it: tall, ruddy, clean-shaven, with green eyes so bright that the women lowered theirs when they went by him, even if he were paying no attention to them. Military life had given him the air of a conqueror, but of things far more serious than mere women. As soon as he arrived, he had gone up to the doctor's to thank him, bringing him a young kid and an invitation to the famous shearing. The doctor spoke to him in dialect; he answered in proper Italian. And when the doctor asked, rather pointedly: "Are you inviting many people?" he answered: "Yes, because it's a big family, and a man like me – well, I may have many enemies, but I also have many friends. Besides, I'm broad-minded, and I'm inviting even the relatives of Lenarda's first husband. They can kill me, if I'm lying. And if she had had three husbands, I'd invite the relatives of them all."

"You're a man of the world, I see. Good for you. I suppose you'll invite your neighbors, too."

Being a man of the world, Jacu pretended to know nothing of the doctor's madness over Zana.

"Of course, a neighbor is more than a relative."

The day of the shearing came, and Zana, Zia Lenarda, and the other women took seats in the cart that Jacu drove.

The sheepfold was on the plateau, and the heavy vehicle, drawn by two black steers, scarcely broken, bounced up along the rocky path; but the women weren't afraid, and Zana, her hands clasping her knees, was calmly crouched down as if in front of her own hearth. She seemed sad, but her eyes gleamed with a kind of hidden lightening, like a far–off blaze, shining on a dark night in the heart of a forest.

"Neighbor," Jacu said good-humoredly, "hang me, but you have a face like a funeral. He'll come, he'll come. He's coming later, with the priest, as soon as mass is over...."

"Cheer up, Zana," the women said then, joking a little maliciously, "I hear a horse now, trotting like the devil himself."

"Cheer up, girl. I can see his watch chain shining."

"What a chain that is! How much would that chain cost? Nine *reali?*"

Then Zana grew angry. "Evil take you all. Leave me alone. I can't bear him. The crows can pluck out my eyes if I even look at that man's face today...."

The doctor and the priest arrived a little before noon, welcomed with shouts of joy. In the shade of a cork tree Jacu, the servant, and his friends sheared the sheep, laying them out, carefully bound, on a broad stone that looked like a sacrificial altar. The dogs chased one another through the grass, birds chirped in the oak, an old man who looked like the prophet Elijah gathered the wool into a sack, and all around the asphodel and the wild lilies, bent by the scent-laden wind, seemed to lean forward, curious to see what was happening in the midst of that group of men who stooped down, the shears in their hands. Once they were sheared and released, the sheep jumped up from the heap of wool, as from a foaming wave, and bounded off, shrunken, their muzzles rubbing the earth.

For a while the doctor stood watching, his hands clasped behind him, then he turned to the hut, where the women were cooking, assisted by Jacu's old father, who reserved for himself the honor of roasting a whole kid on the spit. Farther on, the priest, stretched out on the grass in the shade of another cork tree, was telling a Boccaccian tale to a select group of youths. The women nudged Zana and pointed to the doctor; and all at once, with a change of mood, she began to joke with him, asking him to make himself useful at least, by going to get some water at the spring. He went along with her jokes and, taking a cork pail, walked off in the bright sunlight that scorched the grass and the sage and made a perfume that was enough to intoxicate a man.

The group around the priest sent whistles and shouts after the doctor, and the old man roasting the kid caught his thumb in his fingers as a gesture of contempt. A learned man, a grown man, letting himself be made a fool of like this by the women! Then Zana cursed and ran off, holding her kerchief to her head, until she caught up with the doctor and took the pail out of his hand. From a distance, the women saw the man follow her along the path that led to the spring and Jacu's old father began to spit furiously on the fire, as if he wanted to put it out.

"The granddaughter of Tomas Acchittu – you see her? She wanted to be alone with the man. If she was my daughter, I'd put my foot on her neck."

"Let her be, father-in-law," Zia Lenarda said kindly. Ah, she knew what love was, how it made you mad, like drinking bewitched water.

The doctor, in fact, dazed by the bright sun, followed Zana into the thicket around the spring and again he tried to take her in his arms. She looked at him with those eyes of hers, like the Queen of Sheba's; but she pushed him away, threatening to pour the pail full of water on his head.

Always the same, since the first evening there by the low wall of the courtyard; she led him on and repulsed him, half ingenuous, half treacherous, and asked him always for the same thing: some poison.

"All right, then, Zana, I'll make you happy. Tonight I'll come to your house, and I'll bring one of those little bottles with a skull on it. But be careful you don't end in jail."

"It's for the fox, I tell you. All right, but leave me now. You hear? Someone's coming."

In fact, the thicket around the fountain shook as if a boar were crashing through, then Jacu appeared. His face was overwrought, although he pretended that finding the two of them was a joke.

"Hey! What are you doing there in the dark? It's time to eat, not to be courting...."

"You're not so hungry, you're thirsty," Zana said sarcastically, lifting the pail, "have a drink, handsome...."

But Jacu threw himself full-length on the ground and drank, panting, from the spring.

During the banquet the doctor laughed, while the priest threw bread crumbs at him and hinted maliciously. He laughed, but from time to time he was distracted, struck by a new idea. After the banquet was over he went off to lie down in the shade among the rocks behind the hut; from there he could see without being seen, and he commanded a view of the area down to the oak in whose shade the shepherd went on shearing. The priest and the others, nearer by, had begun a singing contest, and the women were listening, seated in a row, their hands in their laps.

In the intense silence, the voices, the songs, the laughter were dispelled like the thin white clouds in the blue vastness; and the doctor could hear a horse cropping the grass beyond the rocks, a dog gnawing a bone inside the hut, where Jacu came every so often to empty the sheared wool.

All at once Zana, as the song contest grew more lively, got up and came into the hut. The doctor was smoking; he observed the blue thread that rose from his cigar, and a kind of grin raised his upper lip, showing the gold fillings of his teeth.

Finally Jacu arrived, and Zana's choked voice came like a moan through the cracks in the hut.

"I swear...may I be eaten by the hawks...if he's even touched my hand. I have my own reasons for smiling at him....It's all for our own good....But this suffering will end...end...."

The man, intent perhaps on emptying the wool, was silent. She went on, exasperated, her voice filled with hate: "What about me? Am I ever jealous of your wife? The old crow, the fox. But it's going to end...soon...."

Then Jacu laughed; and again there was heard the laughter, the singing, the grazing horse.

But the doctor wanted to enjoy himself a little. He leaped to his feet and began to shout: "Hey! a fox! a fox!"

And the two lovers ran out of the hut, amazed, while below, the group stopped their singing, the women looked all around them, and the dogs started to bark as if a fox had really gone past.

Translated by William Weaver

CARNIVAL TIME
by
Paola Drigo

Ursule, Teresine, and Catinùte leapt up and ran to open the door. A comical-looking group burst in, jumping and dancing their way into the kitchen. There were five or six players in masks obviously homemade but meant to be scary or grotesque. One was fiery red and with charcoal markings, and it was meant to represent the devil. A second one consisted of an extremely long nose protruding above an equally long raggedy beard of coarse fibers. A third one had a pig's snout. The others in the troupe had been content with sticking a colored rag or a piece of paper fringe onto their everyday clothes, or simply turning their jackets inside out and putting nightcaps on their heads.

The devil vaulted about like a young stag. The old man walked on his hands with his head down and his legs in the air. As for the pig, he sang crowing cock-a-doodle-doo with the voice of a rooster. They were youths from the neighboring farms, habitual visitors of the *filò*, and probably rivals amongst themselves for the girls, linked by the common desire to "celebrate carnival time."

The merry party was led by a slim blond fellow without a mask, a bit lame, calm and collected, who had a fine accordion with painted decorations slung across his shoulders. With a vigorous pulling out of the bellows, he launched into a dancing tune and the cue for a song.

39

It was a magnificent success. And since supper was finished anyway, everyone, except the two older men and Barbe Zef intent on draining the last wine from a jug, quit the kitchen and amid laughing remarks and applause moved out into the barn with the new arrivals.

The barn was newly whitewashed, roomy, and well tended. Thirty or so reddish-brown cows with albino eyes, small but with sleek hides, populated it along with their numerous calves, and they spread throughout its interior a rather moist and heavy warmth. Along the walls narrow wooden benches, a few rough-hewn tables, and some chairs had been prepared for the *filò*. The lighting, consisting of two old kerosene lanterns hung from the ceiling, was not excessively bright, but the company made do with it.

Before everyone could find a suitable place to stand or sit – and in the company that he or she preferred – there was a moment of confusion and jostling during which the hunchback, with the pretext of escorting her, was at Mariutine's heels rubbing up against her as much as he could. He squeezed her elbow, he touched her arm, and with a blade of straw he tickled her on the neck, but as though by accident and without ulterior motive, eyeing her, as though inadvertently, out of the corner of his eye.

And all at once, above the uproar, there resounded a blast of nose-blowing, long and penetrating like the summons blared out by a hunting horn.

"Make way! Make way!" he set up a shrill shout, his sharp voice in falsetto.

At once the crowd drew back along the walls, and the accordion player lit into a spirited mazurka. Compare Guerrino, tossing his hat in the air and catching hold of Mariutine's waist, went spinning off into the middle of the little crowd of spectators. Although for a hunchback he was strangely tall and very long-legged, his head hardly came up as high as Mariutine's breast, and yet he lifted her almost up into the air and whirled her around so dizzily that it seemed as though her feet never touched the ground.

They danced the famous "toe and heel" mazurka, in great esteem in that part of the countryside, with its intricate steps and innumerable variations. Mariutine had had virtually no opportunities to dance it, but she danced by instinct like most of the mountain girls once she had overcome her initial shyness, and she rushed ahead confident and light on her feet, gracefully following her partner. He, gripping her like a spider, "led" her in masterful style, with the trippings, turns, and virtuosities of a consummate artist. He stamped his heel, throwing up his foot shod in a kind of shoe that passed for citified, the toe pointed upward. He opened his legs like a compass and closed them again with a click. His humped back was no trouble to him, nor did the years seem to weigh on him, for he could not have been less than fifty or fifty-five years old. The tails of his jacket flew out, matched in the same rhythms by the fluttering out of Mariutine's smock and skirts.

The company had abruptly withdrawn its attention from the masked entertainers to focus on the dancing. At every tricky step, at every unexpected and original variation, a murmur of approval arose, and some enthusiast couldn't help exclaiming, "They're neat, by gosh! They're neat!"

When at last, with a full and throbbing chord, the mazurka came to an end, they all clapped their hands. A shepherd-boy brought the hunchback his hat, in which he had stuck a long rooster feather, a sign of primacy, and the cry "Music! Music!" resounded on all sides.

At once the devil with his fiery red, ugly face, the old man with the long white beard, and the fellow with the pig's snout who had given up his cock-a-doodle-doo, with great seriousness, knowing that they had an obligation to dance well, took Ursule, Teresine, and Catinùte out onto the dance floor. They began to wheel about in rhythm with the music, in their heavy hobnailed shoes.

Meanwhile Compare Guerrino had not let go of Mariutine, and he urged her with great familiarity towards a corner of the barn where there was a low stool. Panting and out of breath, he wiped the sweat dripping down his forehead with a large red kerchief. Mariutine too was overheated. One of her braids had come loose, and her heart was beating as after a fast race. Yet she felt happy and proud of her well-earned success. Nor did it ever enter her mind to regret having had an older, hunchbacked partner instead of a handsome young man. She took her place cheerily enough beside Compare Guerrino, and she smiled at him gratefully.

They were silent for a bit. A cluster of people separated them like a wall from the space allotted to dancing. No one paid attention to them. Only two white calves from their place close by turned around to look at them placidly. Finally the hunchback, continuing to pass the kerchief over his deadly pale and sweaty face, without looking at his companion, said nonchalantly, "You can't be all that well off up there in that hole where you live. Why don't you find a job in town?"

The question touched a spot too sensitive for Mariutine, excited by the dance and by all the extraordinary events of that whole day though she was, to hear it calmly. She suddenly felt whisked away from the joy and heedlessness of the moment and brought back to the dark foreboding that had made up the fear and menace of her entire life. She started up and blushed furiously; nevertheless, by a great effort conquering her bashfulness, she answered: "I'd rather have a hard time up there at our place, than go be a servant . . ." she murmured with lowered eyes, but firmly. "And then, even if I wanted to, I couldn't."

"Why couldn't you?"

"I have to take care of Barbe and my sister."

The hunchback laughed. "As for Barbe, he's old enough to look out for himself. But what do you mean...your sister! How old is she?"

"She's going on seven."

"And where is she now?"

He seemed to have forgotten Rosute's tragedy completely.

"At the hospital in Forni. We brought her there this morning, but she'll soon be cured and she'll be released."

"Ah, ah, she'll be released..." repeated the hunchback two or three times as if he were talking to himself. "She'll be released."

And after a long pause, he continued breezily, "In town, my dear, in the evening, hundreds and hundreds of lights go on all by themselves as though by a miracle, and at night it's as bright as by day. Down there people don't trudge along as we do up here in the midst of snow stones and crags, but they walk on streets smooth as velvet, and, if it rains, they take shelter beneath the porticoes. In town there is music in the square at least twice a week, and people go to the movies and the theater. At carnival time they dance on a platform all festooned with artificial flowers and many-colored balloons, and hundreds of maskers, not scraggly like these, but splendid ones dressed in silk and velvet, offer sugar-almonds to the pretty girls."

And since Mariutine proved interested despite herself and turned her wide-open ingenuous eyes to him in utter fascination, he continued.

"Think about it, beautiful," he said in a low and insinuating voice. "Why don't you want to try it?... And, if ever you do, remember Compare Guerrino. I have occasion to go down to town two or three times a month, and I have many connections. We could find a respectable family, that would treat you as a daughter.... Or perhaps a lady living alone, or better yet, a widower or an elderly bachelor.... A master is always less fussy and demanding than a mistress. I might even know of somebody just right for you.... Such a person, you see, would be someone safe for you to rely on. He wouldn't treat you badly. The one I have in mind knows what young people need. Is that clear? If ever you feel like doing it, just let me know somehow. And meanwhile think about it. Will you do that?"

"You're very kind, Compare Guerrino, and I don't know how to thank you...," murmured the confused girl. "As for thinking about it, I will do that, you can be sure, but, as I've told you...."

"Ta ta ta," the hunchback interrupted her sharply. "I've just been telling you these things for the sake of saying them. You have to have something to talk about. By the way, how old are you?"

"Fifteen."

"That's young. You look at least four years older. You already have such breasts! While dancing I felt them, you know? And what a sweet scent you have – really of a fresh rose, or a musk rose."

44

As he made these remarks Compare Guerrino's tongue licked his lips and he looked at the girl hungrily. His eyes lingered on her budding breasts that were still lightly heaving, on her thighs that could be readily guessed at as they were outlined under her thin skirt, and on her red and fleshy mouth.

"You're the most beautiful *fantate* I've ever seen," he murmured, pressing against her on the low stool.

Mariutine blazed up in blushes. She felt diffident toward the hunchback because he was her elder and because he was the master, and even if she had known how, she would not have dared to reply, for her extreme poverty had shaped in her ever since early childhood the habit of compliance and almost of servility with regard to anyone outside of her own family. But these were the first praises, the first compliments ever, that had come to her coarsely directed toward her physical self. More than flattering her, they caused her deep embarrassment, just as did Compare Guerrino's speeches and familiarity, which while they interested and amused her, also aroused an obscure sense of discomfort.

Just then, abruptly raising her eyes as though summoned by other eyes, she met the gaze of Barbe Zef, who had entered the barn unannounced. Crouched on his heels next to a table where they were gambling, behind a cluster of people, he was eying Mariutine and her companion closely. On meeting the girl's gaze, he swiftly shifted his eyes and pretended to be following the game. Mariutine had noticed the whole scene, but she did not make anything of it. And the hunchback too perhaps had noticed, for, without paying any further attention to her and without a word of good-bye, he got up and left his place with an indifferent air.

Joining the people who made up the *filò*, lingering first with this one and then with the other, tossing off a joke here, a compliment there, and a sardonic word further on, distributing to the shepherd–boys little tweaks of the ear and to the girls fond little pinches, like a king holding court he passed the entire company in review. Swarthy, unattractive, and deformed as he was, he nevertheless had the manner of the true master, and in his eyes there was an astute and intelligent expression. When he reached Barbe Zef, he turned to him with a joke, and Barbe Zef replied quietly and with deference, without the remotest trace of awkwardness. Then Compare Guerrino, at the center of a small circle of men, tight-lipped and without laughing, began to tell a story, spicy certainly and bold, for Barbe Zef and the other older men, already leering after the glasses of wine they had drunk, could be seen splitting their sides with laughter.

Meanwhile the young men of the family and after them the other youths, as soon as they saw Mariutine free from Compare Guerrino's escort, rushed to invite her to dance. And she, her eyes agleam like two blue pearls, rosy and disheveled, passed from one to the next, light on her feet and radiant with joy.

The dancers kept it up until nearly midnight, when, inexplicably, there was a sudden pause and a silence. Then without need for a word of agreement, men, women and children, and even the white-haired old men, all bounded up on their feet at the same time, and unfurling their voices they joined in a chorus:

The sun at sunset is a glory
And the moon splendid above
And the stars they form a crown
And sweethearts are making love.

It was the traditional chorus that concluded the
filò. But even apart from that, the shepherd-boys
who were falling asleep, the platters of chestnuts
where nothing more remained than the shells, the
empty pitchers, and the languishing conversations
were all signs clearly indicating that the evening
was over.

The visitors, led by the lame accordionist, were
saying their good-byes. Since Barbe Zef and
Mariutine would have to be leaving the next day at
dawn to make the return journey to their high land,
the thanks and leave-takings of the family were
exchanged on the spot before everybody disbanded
to go to bed.

Ursule invited Mariutine to sleep with them in
their bed. Barbe Zef had a good pallet and a heavy
blanket in the barn. The others, after innumerable
"mandis" and handclasps, went off on their own.

In the little bedroom, the girls quickly got
undressed, while through the nocturnal silence the
drawn-out tones of the receding accordion continued to reach their ears:

Oh my dearest Ursuline,
Oh my dusky darling one,
Black your curls and sweet your mouth,
Created just for making love.

Translated by Blossom S. Kirschenbaum

DEAR GIUSEPPE
by
Natalia Ginzburg

Dear Giuseppe,

All of a sudden I've a great desire to write to you. So I've locked the door to my room so that no one can come and annoy me while I'm writing to you.

It's five in the afternoon and it's very hot. Everyone's in a bad mood, perhaps because of the heat. A short while ago there was a great row between my mother-in-law and the Swiss girl, because my mother-in-law went into the Swiss girl's room and the bed had not been made yet and she saw that the mattress was stained with menstrual blood. Then she saw biscuit crumbs and ants under the bed.

This row irritated me. I found both of them unbearable. The Swiss girl said she would leave tomorrow and took her suitcases down from the top of the wardrobe. I tried to calm her down but without success. If she leaves tomorrow I shall have everything to manage – the children and the house at a time when I want to just stay quietly in my room and think.

So many things have happened to me since you left. My life has changed. I've fallen in love. You will be surprised if I tell you that I've never been in love before, when I always kept telling you that I fall in love very easily, but they were all mistakes, and perhaps you'll be offended if I tell you that you

were a mistake too. I thought I was in love with
you, I thought I wanted to live with you – what a
mistake, Giuseppe – you, thank goodness, were
terrified at the prospect and told me for God's sake
to stay where I was. You were wise and I thank you
for it. I got on with you well enough, at the beginning. I felt happy enough, but it was all on the
level of enough. When I met you my life did not
change color. Now it has changed color. Piero
accepted you, he stayed calm, more or less, my
adultery with you was a bloodless affair. Now, on
the contrary, my adultery is of the kind that scatters
blood all over the place. I.F. and I are madly in
love with each other and we are going to live
together, I don't know when. I don't know where.
We shall get a house in a town, I don't know which
one. I shall take the children with me. You were
afraid of the children, he isn't, he isn't afraid of
anything.

When I saw him arrive here the first time and get
out of his olive-green Renault and come towards
me with that gray crewcut he has, I suddenly felt
scared and irritated. I said to myself, "Now who in
God's name can this be?" We paused for a moment
and looked at each other, not moving, face to face.
We are about the same height – I'm a very little
taller than he is, but only a very little. The dogs
started barking. They didn't want him there.
Egisto and Albina were behind him and they were
surprised that the dogs were barking, usually they
don't bark. From that moment I have liked Egisto
and Albina even more and I really enjoy seeing
them. He went into the house and hung his raincoat
on the coatstand and immediately a nail came out
of the wall and the coatstand came crashing down.
Goodness knows why a nail should come out of the
wall at that precise moment. Afterwards I told him

that the dogs barking and the coatstand coming down had been two omens.

I think that Piero quickly realized that something was going on because his manner changed immediately, from the first few times that I.F. started coming here on Saturdays he seemed always frightened and upset. At first he only came on Saturday, but then on other days during the week too. He would phone and then come over. Now he doesn't come any more. Sometimes we meet in Pianura and go for a walk in the country. But usually I go to his house in Rome. He has a relationship with that woman called Ippolita, though everyone calls her Ippo. They don't live together. She's a woman with a big nose and beautiful hair. Everybody tells me about her hair. Everybody – Albina, Egisto – tells me about it. What on earth's so marvelous about her hair! I've never seen her. Egisto's seen her, he's been in her house. She has a very beautiful terrace. Everybody talks about her terrace too. I.F. finds it difficult to leave her because it will hurt her, he hasn't told her anything about me, but in a few days now he's going to tell her about me and leave her. It hasn't been easy for me to talk to Piero either, but I had to talk to him because I would have felt bad if I hadn't talked to him. Anyway, Piero had already realized everything. He's very depressed. We had an open relationship – you remember that we were always saying so – but in fact it was only open on my side, Piero has never loved any other woman but me. Anyway an open relationship reaches a point when it either closes or goes to pieces. The relationship between Piero and me is going to pieces. I'm sorry because I'm fond of Piero, I'm sorry to see him depressed. I feel that he wouldn't have been so depressed if I had gone off with you, but he thinks

of I.F. as something dreadful. He always comes
home very late from Perugia and eats alone; I sit
myself down at the table while he's eating and he
tells me to go away. He can't stand me and I can't
stand him. We sleep together but on some nights I
tell him I'm too hot and I go and sleep upstairs in
the room that has the quilts with dragons on them.
It should be cooler in there because it faces west,
but in fact it's stiflingly hot in there too. Sometimes I'm very unhappy as well.

The strange thing is that everything is breaking
up here, the whole house is falling to pieces. The
Swiss girl is leaving tomorrow, the washing machine leaks. It's very hot, we're all dead with the
heat. The Swiss girl used to take the children to
the stream every day, but she's going tomorrow and
I shall have to take them because if I don't they will
wander round the garden getting bored and filthy.
Serena has gone to Russia, otherwise she could
have taken them to the stream. I think the children
have realized something is going on too, because
they all seem frightened and bored. Perhaps the
Swiss girl has realized too and that's why she's
going, because it isn't very cheerful staying
somewhere where everything's falling to pieces.
Only my mother-in-law hasn't realized anything.
Every so often she comes to me with a worried look
on her face and tells me that she has found a dead
bird full of ants on the bathroom windowsill, or she
tells me she's found a bowl of moldy figs in the
refrigerator. Whenever my mother-in-law goes
round the house these days she always finds
something disgusting.

You are really my only friend. And so I'm very
very sorry that you're so far away just at the time
when I need to confide in someone. Serena isn't
here now either. But then I'm not so sure that

Serena would listen to me and understand. I think she would immediately take Piero's side. Her head's always full of the position of women, women's rights, etc., but I know only too well that she would despise me. Sometimes I talk to Albina when she comes on Saturdays. I tell her something, not everything, of how things stand. But my one real friend is you. And you have to go and hole yourself up in America. Our long affair has left us with a deep friendship for each other. I feel it for you and I hope you feel it for me. We've also had a son together, Graziano. You don't want me to say so but it's true. A son together and a deep friend‑ship. These are the good things I have given to you and which you have given to me, the good things that we own together. You don't give a damn about your son and you pretend he has nothing to do with you – as you wish, it doesn't matter. But I think you will acknowledge our friendship as real.

Your son Alberico came here once. But after‑wards so many things happened that I forgot to tell you about it. I don't know if I like this son of yours. I don't understand him very well. He gave his name to that girl's baby. Of course he did it to be the opposite of you, to be what you don't want to be, the father of a child coming into the world.

Send me your news. And tell me what's happen‑ing to you. Let me know if you're still sleeping in the room with the bear cubs.

Lucrezia

*

Giuseppe to Lucrezia
Princeton, 4th August

Dear Lucrezia,

Your letter moved me a great deal, so much so that I couldn't work for the whole day. You know I'm writing a novel, I think I've mentioned it to you. Your letter got so tangled up with my thoughts that I couldn't free myself from it, and I found your face and your voice everywhere inside me. I didn't answer immediately. I let a few days pass, because it upset me to answer you.

You are in love with Ignazio Fegiz, or with I.F. as you call him. This should not mean anything to me, or rather it should please me, because falling in love is a splendid thing and because a person is pleased if something splendid happens to someone he is fond of. Instead, I felt uneasy as I read your letter. You want to leave Piero and go and live with I.F. and take your children with you. You tend to think of your children as if they were furniture or luggage. Besides, there are five of them, not just one. If there were one you could put everything into reassuring him. But it's not easy to reassure five children. And for I.F., too, five children is not going to be a small undertaking. You say that "he's not afraid of anything." As for yourself I have to tell you that at the very least I think you are being reckless. And I have to think the same about him.

What you say about us, about you and me, "our adultery was a bloodless affair," seems ridiculous to me. No adultery is bloodless. And then according to you we have had a son together. I don't think that's true, but if it is true our adultery was not a bloodless affair. Children are blood, and they are born surrounded by blood.

I felt there was something lurking behind your whole letter, something that hurt me deeply, an ob-

53

scure desire to compare I.F. and me with each other, and to see me as someone inferior, less noble, less valued. Your dogs barked for him. The coatstand fell down for him. Then you say that he is about the same height as you. You know very well that I hardly come up to your shoulders, and that this always upset me.

You say "I got on with you well enough, I felt happy enough, it was all on the level of enough." How nasty you can be. How cruel. You know how to make someone suffer. I don't believe that you don't know.

As for your dithyrambs about our friendship, I have to tell you that I find them hard to believe, and so I don't know how to respond to them. Real friendship does not scratch and bite, and your letter scratched and bit me.

What shall I tell you about myself. I get along well. Well enough. On the level of enough, of course. I'm content. The school is closed at the moment. I'm on holiday. I start again in September. I'm writing my novel. Anne Marie gets back from the Institute around six in the evening. I watch her while she's making the dinner, a complicated dinner, big rissoles that have to be cooked slowly, with carrots and stock, soups made with beetroot and cream. Russian dishes that I've learnt to love. Anne Marie had a Russian grandmother. We say very little. Anne Marie is someone who says very little, and always in a low voice, and I like that. I find it restful to live with someone who weighs her words, who speaks sparingly and judiciously. Anne Marie smiles all the time and I have learnt to smile all the time too while she is there. Sometimes my mouth is a little tired with the effort of all that smiling. But I think that little by little we shall finally stop smiling.

No, I don't sleep in the room with the bear cubs.
I sleep upstairs. But I don't sleep with Anne Marie,
if that's what you want to know.

Giuseppe

*

Piero to Giuseppe
Monte Fermo, 25th August

Dear Giuseppe,
  I haven't had any reply to a letter I wrote you
about two months ago. Perhaps you didn't receive
it, or perhaps you didn't think it necessary to answer me. The latter seems more likely to me. At
the moment I tend to think no one can be bothered
with me.
  Lucrezia has gone. I don't know where she's
gone, she didn't tell me. I'm alone in this house
which I loved so much, and which I now hate. My
mother and children are away. I don't know where
Lucrezia is. It's terrible to think about someone all
the time and not know where she is. She just
jumped into her Volkswagen one morning. I saw
her swimming flippers sticking out of her bag. I
asked her where she was going and she said she
didn't know. She said she would phone me. I asked
her if she had enough money and she said she had.
It's been eight days now and she hasn't phoned yet.
  I get in my car every morning and go to Perugia.
I haven't got anything to do at the office but I go
there just the same. At least it's air-conditioned
there. Doctor Corsi is on holiday and so are both
our secretaries. I eat in a little café nearby. This is
what my life is going to be like when Lucrezia has
gone for good.
  She told me she would take the children with
her. I told her I would never allow her to. This
isn't true, I know very well that she will do what-

55

ever she's decided on. She has a strong character. I'm a weak person. I've trailed this feeling of being weak around with me since I was a child. She will give me the children one day a week and for a month in the summer. It happens like this for lots of people, lots of men. Normally when a marriage goes to pieces the women take the children. In the summer the children will be with me. I won't know what to say to them, because you don't know what to say to children when they're with you for one month a year. There are too many things you want to tell them, and they stick in your throat. I think that during that month one would try and be as kind and easygoing as possible so that they will love you and have good memories of you throughout the winter. I think that this effort to be kind and easygoing with your own children must be very exhausting. And it must be something that makes you feel contemptible. And then it's a mistake because children don't like an easygoing atmosphere. They like to have strict, authoritative people around them. People suspect it's a mistake, but they do it anyway. That's what I shall do too.

You had a long relationship lasting several years with Lucrezia. This will seem strange to you, but it never upset me. I stayed calm. I knew that we weren't going to be hurt by it. You're not someone who hurts people, you are someone who is careful not to hurt people as he goes by, not to trample on or destroy anything. You and I are birds of a feather. You are one of those who always loses.

I realize that I've written without giving you any explanation, as if you already knew everything. But I imagine that Lucrezia has already told you. We have decided to separate. Or rather, she has decided. I haven't decided anything. I bowed my head and accepted.

My mother will come back in a few days. She
and I will be alone. The children are all at Forte
dei Marmi at the moment, with my sister. My
mother doesn't know anything. I shall have to tell
her and I dread it. She will cry, she'll be full of
pity for me and it's very difficult to put up with
pity from one's parents. It's much easier to put up
with pity from one's children. Goodness knows
why.

My mother will cry. I shall have to comfort her.
I shall have to tell her that I'm all right.
Reasonably all right. I shall have to tell her that
these things often happen.

I'm always thinking of you.

Yours,
Piero

*

Giuseppe to Piero
Princeton, 30th August

Dear Piero,

I had heard what you wrote to me from Lucrezia.

I did get your other letter. I didn't reply not
because I didn't think it necessary to answer you,
but because I found it difficult to do so, as I had
sensed from a distance things that you didn't
mention, and as I had had letters from Lucrezia that
said everything.

Even now it's not easy for me to write to you and
tell you what I went through as I read your last
letter. It isn't easy to tell you how close I feel to
you in this disaster that's overtaken you. I think of
it as a disaster for both of you, even though only
you are suffering at the moment, and she perhaps is
happy, or thinks she is.

I'm sorry not to be with you at Monte Fermo, not
to go for walks with you in the woods and over the

little hills there as we have done so many times. You know that you have a loyal friend in me, even though in the past I betrayed you – though we stayed friends – in the way you know about. It's not that I'm someone who is careful not to hurt anyone as he goes by, not to trample on or destroy things. It's not true. I have destroyed and trampled underfoot a great many things that were in my way. In fact when I get up in the morning I find in myself a deep disgust for what I am, for my feet in their slippers, for my sad face in the mirror, for my clothes draped over the chair. As the day goes on this disgust becomes gradually more and more stifling.

As you know I'm not returning to Italy for the moment. I'm writing a novel and I want to finish it. Besides, I have a relationship here with someone, a strange relationship that's quite different from all the others I've previously had with women. It's a woman I'm talking about. It's Anne Marie, my brother's widow. My brother was very fond of her and for this reason I am very fond of her. But she and I don't talk to each other, or we say very little. It's a relationship of smiles and murmurs. It's a relationship that seems calm, but inwardly it is shaken by continual shocks.

I too am always thinking of you.

Yours,
Giuseppe

Translated by Dick Davis

THE FRENCH TEACHER
by
Geda Jacolutti

Ne jetez aucun object par la fênetre.
Do not throw anything out of the window.
In junior high school all my classmates were in love with the French teacher.

At that time refined and vampish men were the fashion and our French teacher interpreted the type with a lavish style and a little disengagé. In class the girls watched him in fascination, madness. I observed the desk and the actor who rested his moist, pseudo-distracted look upon us from the platform and, annoyed at seeing how the others admired him, I found it easier to play the insolent student. He spoke slowly, in a nasal voice, putting out his half-smoked cigarette before beginning to read a poet, and from time to time interrupting his reading to make some ironic or sentimental comment. The girls gazed at his eyes and hair and whispered "a mouth to bite" among themselves, according to the manner of that age. I chose the moment of highest enchantment to act: I let a dictionary crash to the floor with a calculated clatter and responded with dry provocation to the rebuke from the desk.

Ganeglio jumped and turned excitedly to look at me. She was the most inflamed of the enamored group and spent the hour trying to find a pretext to go up to his desk or start a conversation, and she was even willing to be questioned without being prepared.

One day she was hanging around near his desk when the teacher began to ask her questions about the lesson. Ganeglio, who studied very little, didn't even try to answer, and began looking at him with mischievous eyes, but he was insistent. So she leaned against the wall, and with her eyes closed she sighed. Then in submissive tones she breathed, "Professor, leave me alone," amid the snickers of the boys and to the embarrassment of her companions who were ashamed for her.

Anyway Ganeglio was very provocative and broad-minded. She was a skater and wore very short skirts, but she was also a practicing Catholic who often went to confession, describing to the confessor the type of kisses she had received from her fiancé (there seemed to be three different categories involved and one had to pay close attention to what was permitted and what was not). The next day between classes she would avidly tell us all the details of her confession.

I couldn't listen to her; I would have burst into childish laughter, but I was no longer the age for that, so I would just return home in a fury.

In the afternoons I spent hours translating Greek and Latin with ritualistic persistence. I relished my severe aloneness, and modelled my will on the lives of illustrious men. Casual glances at the mirror reflected the image of a too thin face with heavy, smoothly-combed braids. The sternness of that face made me proud. And yet I sometimes surprised myself when, looking out the window at the sky broken by chimney tops, a dizzy void would sud-

denly open up in my heart. Then it was as if my
future life fell unknown and fearful upon me; and
when my mother's voice called me to supper, I
would start with the sensation of having been
caught crossing a forbidden boundary.

It happened one morning during recess when we
were in high school. The halls were crowded as
usual and swarming with the many troops of boys
running around, cutting up and laughing boister-
ously.

We girls were chatting as we leaned against a
radiator in front of a locker room, a place we
considered our territory for our own uninterrupted
use. It was then I saw the French teacher cross the
hall calmly and quietly in the midst of the uproar of
those awkward adolescents, and I realized I hadn't
seen him for months, not since I had graduated from
junior high school. Released from the conventional
role that we had assigned him, he looked for a
moment like a stranger, and at the same time he
seemed an old friend who had for years taught me
to read and study with a taste both sharp and a bit
nonchalant.

An old friend, now I saw it clearly, and I also
clearly saw his age. He was a little bent and
seemed tired, and that silent and courteous passage
suddenly put him in a generation far removed from
mine. I felt a sharp pain together with guilt for
having caught those signs of aging by surprise.

That pain returned to bother me later, when I
realized that I was thinking about him, and curious
about what was happening to me I began to reflect
upon myself, upon my soul. Inadvertently I was
opening the door to a sickness of the imagination
(even now I cannot call it sentiment), to a sickness

that was to condition my life and my choices for many years.

During the day my actions, interests, conversation, were completely like those of my contemporaries: the new dress, the tennis game, school work, but in the evenings I filled the pages of my diary well into the night. My desires were naive and literary and the model for them was derived from famous examples, but the hold that that feeling had on me sprang from a kind of intellectual intensity that grew in strength as I continued writing, and from an exercise of concentration that made everything inside and outside me real and new.

All I ever dreamed of was a contemplative life where I was the anchorite and he the object of adoration. His handwriting discovered in an old notebook acquired the power of a talisman from which inexhaustible images, situations, traces of memory emanated. But I know for certain that I never thought of that sentiment as an attainable project; there was only one thing I was unable to accept: that that fervor could, with the passage of time, be extinguished in me; it would have been like accepting the loss of a part of my soul.

Besides, nearly all the young men of my own age seemed clumsy and unkempt, and I didn't understand how anyone could like them. I thought that only in the tranquil fullness of maturity was it possible to be in "control of the situation," and therefore among my contemporaries I was only interested in those who made a pretense of being mature, sophisticated, skeptical – the exact opposite of what I really wanted. I didn't know then that men seldom reached a tranquil maturity, and I took it for granted that the French teacher had.

But the reason for that, which I certainly did not know at the time (knowing too little about psychology), was perhaps because he was exactly the age of my father.

And so for many years he was my standard of reference. Even when I had finished high school and the opportunities for meeting the French teacher had become rarer (and by now that love was only a memory), I realized that my feelings continued to be due to a kind of forced concentration, on a comparison – not with him, his person or qualities, but with the feeling I had had for him. It seemed to me that without that absolute no feeling could be guaranteed as genuine, and a feeling didn't deserve to be experienced if it wasn't assuredly genuine.

For a good part of my life the desire for love was marked by perplexity, and if that often saved me from disappointments, giving me a kind of consolation at the conclusion of every affair, it also resulted in a discontent with myself, as though I were maimed and incapable of living fully.

But above all, behind those early fantasies I could see openly revealed the insufficiency of reality and the transforming, hypnotic power of the imagination. I wanted to overcome such a state of indecision and subjection, but only much later was I able to, and with much suffering.

When I encountered the French teacher for the last time *(il était très âgé),* he must have been truly old, and yet his style and figure canceled the disagreeable effect of old age.

He was very happy to see me, and we sat at an open air cafe under the trees: the sun was reflected in the glasses and some children were running around and shouting, but his whole person was still wrapped in silence. Then his voice took me back to my adolescence, and for a moment it was as though I heard him call on me from his desk. I noticed that he addressed me by my surname, as he had in class, and I was moved by the affection I sensed in his tone.

I told him that I had been thinking of him the past few days because I was re-reading Stendhal and I remembered how much he loved him, and after all, what I knew I had learned from him.

He sighed as he smiled. "When a person gets old," he said, "he doesn't want to read anything that makes him think. Everything leads to the same reflection, and one...," he hesitated, "one prefers to ignore it."

Then I had the impulse to tell him how much my mind, my life had been taken up with him at one time, but the words I was trying to formulate already seemed like a distorting, showy parody, a grotesque perversion of a feeling that had once been alive and that for so many years I had obstinately tried to find in other faces I had loved.

He saw I was lost in thought and distracted, and fearing he had made me melancholy, he rose to pay for our drink, or rather he went to the counter – as was the custom of his generation – so as not to handle the transaction before a woman.

We said good-bye. Then I watched him, a little stooped, walk away in the sun, and with him the inherent gentility of a generation sunk in time and now completely lost.

Translated by Martha King

TOSCA'S CATS
by
Gina Lagorio

Tosca had just about finished washing the hall. That was the third time the brush wiped the floor to rinse off all the detergent: because the landlady – the Nazi was what she called her while talking to the cats – had accused her of leaving the stairs slippery, "a real hazard for everyone." She was in a sweat more because of that accusation than with the actual effort when she found herself face to face with the journalist, in a linen suit, a briefcase and bag in his hands. His face, made thinner by diet, looked younger with a suntan. They smiled and said good morning to each other in hushed voices, because the horizon was just going pink and the fresh air was still reminiscent of the night.

He was on his way to Rome, a fast drive to the airport, a quick job in the city, and: "I hope I'll be back for the concert tonight. By the way, will you join us? I've got an extra ticket; tell Tonì about it, you can go at least, the two of you, I mean; and if I'm late, I'll join you at Finale."

Tosca blushed with pleasure and gratitude and stammered her thanks. What a kind man! Surely he must have remembered how they had chatted together the previous summer, when she had visited them and talked about the theatrical troupe in Milan, her lifelong passion for the theater and music and how much she missed Corso Garibaldi and Navigli.

She put the brooms and rags away and looked out into the garden: the plants were smiling in the early morning sun; Tosca had given them plenty of water and she was sure they smiled at her after that. Poppa raised her head, looked up at her and meowed. Thank God the little one was attached to its mother's teats.

"I see; thank goodness you've begun to do your duty."

She was pleased with that encounter and walked up the stairs without gasping for breath. On the threshold she found Pussi and Bisi, Poppa's two older kittens, waiting for her. They had gotten into the habit of coming back home more and more often now. The female, Fifi, was more self-sufficient and freer and would stay away for days.

"You've realized there will be no more milk for you, haven't you?" Tosca smiled at seeing them, but at once her voice changed, sounding worried. Pussi had a red line dividing the fur on his head, which was rounder and thicker than his brother's, and he was licking the blood gushing from a deep wound on his forepaw.

Tosca picked him up in her arms and walked into the house followed by Bisi who glided along, his slightly rough fur in constant contact with her legs. From that rough contact which she barely felt, Tosca knew the cat was tense; who knows what had happened to the two of them! If Pussi had been in a bad fight and his brother was sticking to her like that, no doubt they had been in a bad situation together and Bisi was informing her of it in his own way, asking for attention for himself, too. If he had run away leaving his brother alone, Tosca knew that they wouldn't have come back together. She spoke to him fondly and gave them both the food she had prepared. She would take advantage of their eating to treat the injured cat.

It could have been that bossy Mustafà who had dared to defy Miciamore in the past. Now that the whole village, cats included, had joined together to get rid of the only one who could stand up to him, Mustafà was playing the master again. Perhaps he wanted to take revenge on the children for the mortifications suffered from their father. She had seen him wandering in the lane sometimes, but she hadn't bothered about it; now on second thought she realized that the hollow, throaty sound she had heard over and over again at night was Mustafà's call. He was inviting them out, the bastard, challenging them to a fight. Pussi, who was the livelier of the two and the braver as well – she knew it now – must have taken up the challenge. "Poppa would be the answer!" she said loudly, but no animal dared come near Poppa. She was already big, so heavy with her swollen teats; but as soon as a presumed or possible enemy came close, she doubled in size. Lightning seemed about to strike from every single hair, her whiskers stood out on her face, upper lip raised over bared teeth, claws unsheathed. Only when the air ceased to carry the enemy's smell would Poppa withdraw her claws and whiskers and return to a calm state – not without vigilance, however.

Pussi cried and complained when the alcohol got into the wounds, but he didn't run away and Tosca felt proud of him. As a reward, she got a cushion ready for him under the living room win-

dow near a big pot of verbena, his favorite spot.
The cushion had been made soft and pliable to his
body by his father's long use. His brother curled up
close to him; shortly afterwards, as Tosca walked
past them, she noticed the two had reached a fair
agreement: both heads were lying on the pillow,
their bodies were stretched out and almost
perfectly parallel on the floor.

For the millionth time, Tosca thought how much
better it would be to teach children authentic animal behavior rather than some far-fetched poems.
Pascoli's two wolves and the two boys came to
mind.

She had to let Tonì know and yet she felt
embarrassed. She was afraid Tonì would resent her
husband's kindness. Anyway, she should be getting
ready. She had some shampoo and would wash her
hair and look nice and smart: "to make an impression" as Mario used to say when their work day was
over and they both went to the theater or to visit
friends.

Her dress was nice, new, and never worn. It
would have been a surprise for Bruno in the past, if
he had ever even once asked her out to dinner in
some nice place, as she had hoped. The dress had
soft colors with a pattern of large coils looking
like clouds blown across a blue sky. The V-shaped
low neckline showed the beginning of her attractive
breasts. Tosca's legs were still fine and slender,
the large, straight folds of her dress hid her ample
curves. With some makeup, a black lace shawl on
her arm and patent leather sandals, Tonì wouldn't
be ashamed of her.

Tonì wasn't at all upset and was extremely nice when Tosca, after much hesitation, chose to communicate the news by telephone.

When the time came Tosca had been long ready. Tonì called for her to come down; Gigi hadn't arrived yet, the two of them would go on without him.

Tosca felt as she hadn't felt for ages, like a little girl on a holiday. She asked herself why, as she got into Tonì's small car, and the constant rhythm of her heart paused in its beating for an instant. The surprise of that thought had made it stop, and immediately afterwards the rhythmical pace started up in the usual fast, wild gallop.

She laid one hand on her breast, in a gesture that had become habitual, but she didn't worry: the doctor had told her tachycardia was to be expected in a person as sensitive as she was. She was happy because she felt free at last; whenever Bruno came to see her she had been waiting so long, peeping through the shutters, listening for the slightest noise on the stairs, that however happy she was to see him, her happiness was always the exhausted epilogue of a thousand worries, anxiety, guilt feelings, vague (and therefore even more distressing) fears. Now let anyone see her. She had nothing to fear. Nothing to answer for. She relaxed against the back of her seat while Tonì drove fast and confidently on the Via Aurelia not quite yet wrapped in darkness. A slight pink shade still colored the coastline, but the fishermen's boats were already lamp fishing out at sea. She thanked Tonì for the unexpected treat, but Tonì dodged her thanks by shifting the conversation to the performance they were going to attend. If it was something worthwhile, as she hoped, she would review it for her paper.

Tosca asked about her work. She had never read anything by her, or by Gigi either; her pension didn't allow her too many unnecessary expenses. Only once a year she would get some women's magazines when the summer season was over and Giulia, who worked for a hairdresser, passed them on to her. But the weekly paper Tonì wrote theater reviews for was not among them.

It was pleasant to talk to her; she knew everyone – artists, singers, directors – and was on friendly terms with a few of them; maybe during the coming week a party of these people would be their guests on their way to tour France. Tosca was pleased, she knew them too from television and was curious. She asked about this or that one. By the time they parked not far from the open air theater on the outskirts of the small town, they had become better friends. That is what Tosca thought, and again melancholy gave her heart a quick bite. She had forgotten that she too could make a play on words, could ignite some spirited fireworks about a person or event with a flash of imagination. Tonì had laughed more than once at her way of singling out the style of an actor or singer; once her company had been welcome at merry dinner parties in Milan. Even in her solitary house Bruno had often laughed with her, and with her had become interested in something besides his daily tiresome problems.

An unbelievable number of people were packed in the sports ground normally used by schools in wintertime. People even crowded the windows and balconies of the houses surrounding the field like a square.

It was night by then and the lights of Finale seemed so far from the theater. The large blooming hedges bordering the stage added to the illusion of a magic space created for the music. The raised stage was furnished with a grand piano and baskets of flowers.

Expectations for the great tenor ran very high. For years he hadn't performed, but people still loved him. Tosca heard much talk about him from those around her, this one remembered listening to him in an opera in Genoa or Turin, another one had his records, a group behind them – Tosca had noticed they looked smart in a different way, somewhat more sophisticated and expensive – called him a nickname that implied a long-time familiarity. She told Tonì who glanced back after a while and named a few of them in a low voice. Tosca had heard of them; Mario often mentioned them in deep awe: a great actress, a well-known scene painter, a soprano who had sung with Luchino and Callas.

At the tenor's appearance the theater boiled and foamed and rumbled until it thickened into one powerful prolonged applause.

Tosca made herself more comfortable on the chair, the shawl close to her neck as the air had become chilly, and she waited, with a pleasant feeling pervading her whole body, for the music to fill the space between the houses and the people's souls.

"Torna caro ideal" the tenor was singing. He had aged a little, his jacket just a bit too tight over his stout chest. Yet he was still vigorous and self-confident. He could master the audience and lead it wherever he pleased, singing as well as he could

and enjoying the applause no less than when he had sung as he should.

After three songs something special grew between him and the crowd.

A few voices were raised to make a specific request. The nickname the ladies had called him while clapping and shouting "You're still the best!" was used by other people as well. The evening followed a definite "crescendo" movement. The music was an exciting family party for the one who dispensed it and for those who enjoyed it.

Tosca felt relaxed and thrilled at the same time; some sort of joyous fever made her familiar with each note as if it were a message addressed to her only: was life beautiful, could it be again, even for her, why not hope it could?

And she too shouted "Bravo!" when the passionate Neapolitan barcarole that she could remember her mother singing so many times was over.

Tonì was smiling next to her. Sometimes she turned around to see if Gigi had arrived. They found him at the refreshment bar during the break.

"The youngest ones are fifty," Gigi remarked after saying hello to them and Tosca felt resentful. The music had relaxed her and she wasn't afraid to speak her mind.

Tonì took her side and Gigi enjoyed teasing them, complaining about female irrationality. "If it weren't for women, there could have been no romanticism," Tonì burst out, naming glorious poets and artists that Gigi jokingly disposed of as "feminine temperaments."

But after the concert had begun again, even Gigi agreed that Tonì could make a good colorful article "without forgetting," he added, "an ironical touch.

Dress up the enthusiasm with a few sharp remarks or you'll shock your readers under twenty."

"Just the opposite," Tonì retorted, "they are the ones who are after love and romance, my dear. Their ideal, *il caro ideal*, with different music if you like, is always the same."

It was a sweet evening and Gigi took them to a small restaurant where the two women were treated like queens. Tonì explained that restaurant ratings also depended on him. Tosca enjoyed her food more than she had in months.

When they drank a toast at the dessert and Gigi gently touched the arm Tonì had stretched out on the table toward him, Tosca was as moved by that gesture of endearment as if it were meant for her. She quickly lit a cigarette; she wouldn't have let them misunderstand her emotion for anything in the world.

Of this, at least, she was sure: her solitude had not corrupted her to the point of envying people luckier than she. Love, even if it didn't belong to her, was a sweetness in life that she thought of as a blessing to everyone. Something to be thankful for if it touched someone she loved or someone who was simply kind to her.

When she got home Pussi and Bisi were dashing around like elves through the room barely lighted by the glare from the street lights. They were chasing a rubber ball Tosca had had in the house since the days of Miciamore.

She cuddled them, gave them some fresh milk to drink, opened the door in case they wanted to stretch their legs on a night expedition as their father used to do. But those two must have decided that they had had enough of the universe and its risky charms for one day. For a moment they stood uncertainly by the door, their tails upright, then slowly, unhurriedly, they returned to the living room and resumed their play. "Next winter when that woman's no longer here to keep an eye on me, if I know anything about cats, I won't be left without company," Tosca told herself while putting away her silk dress and heading for bed, quite determined to fall asleep without giving in to melancholy thoughts.

Translated by Margherita Piva

THAT ONE DANCE
by
Rosetta Loy

He was enamored, Luis, of Rosetta del Fracin who
was seen in church only at Christmas, at Easter, and
on Palm Sunday to get one of the blessed branches.
She was the daughter of the anarchist blacksmith,
an only girl with five brothers; and with them, in a
large room built of boards stolen from the military
during the upheavals of '21, she raised silkworms.
Her hair was red but her white skin was unblem-
ished by freckles, and when Luis approached the
house down at the Pontisella she emerged from the
putrid silkworm stench in all the splendor of her
clear skin, her cheeks slightly tinged with pink, and
fixed her gaze on him defiantly: what did one of
those sanctimonious Sacarlotts want of her?

But at times she had to turn her head not to laugh
seeing Luis stuck there stiff as a ramrod with his
trousers tight at his ankles and jacket sleeves that
came just a little below his elbows – Sacarlott's
old clothes, ill-adapted for his own size. They
didn't speak to each other because Luis didn't know
what to say and shortly after she would re-enter.
Luis would hear her sing. Her contralto voice was
the Provost's torment, so marvelous would it have
been in the Sanctus or the Hallelujah. Instead,
Rosetta del Fracin sang in a completely different
vein and Luis standing there at the Pontisella felt

his love growing beyond measure. It was both the voice of an angel and an earthly enticement full of mystery because her words were made up then and there and were often senseless.

When summer came Luis did what no one in his family had yet dared: he went to a dance. In their time, the word "dance" had been meaningless to the Sacarlotts, belonging as it did to the vocabulary of either the rich or the demented – the only ones, old Sacarlott said, who could have any wish to go off and tangle their legs in some clownish exhibition after a tiring work day; and his look had frozen anyone who, even vaguely, with some unformed and fanciful desire like the curling of a wave, might have alluded to it. Luis, instead, dug among the old silk shirts given them by Signora Bocca and chose the less yellowed one. He pressed onto his head a little cap of indefinable color, and on the last Sunday of June, in the broiling midday heat, he set out for the Martini farmhouse leaving in distress his mother, his aunt, and his great-aunt.

The Martini place was half-way up the Lu hills and when Luis got there the dance had already begun and Rosetta del Fracin was taken for all of them. But as she saw him from a distance with his cap set back on his curls, she forgot all the promises given and stood stock still under the large, dark leaves of a quince tree, to await him. And barely did Luis approach her than she curved her arms around his neck as if it were already understood they would dance together and Luis became pale, his hands trembled as he clasped her waist and began to swing her around.

They whirled and whirled, and the more Luis tightened his hold the more she let him, and there was a moment when they risked falling to the ground, so tightly clasped were they. Who had taught Luis to dance was not known; perhaps he had learned by himself or maybe it was the great desire to draw the girl to him which gave him all that dash. Certainly his arms quivered and his breath caught; and when he wanted to tell her something and she turned her face close to his mouth, the words died on his lips. But hardly had the music stopped than one of her brothers came and took her off.

Luis danced with la Gramissa, but now dancing with the others didn't matter to him and so he gave them all a turn, even the older ones, married or maiden. The del Fracin brothers had hoisted their sister onto a lame horse to get her home and from there she looked at Luis and it could be read in her large gold-flecked eyes that if he were to return to the place at the Pontisella, it wouldn't be as before. There was in her look, together with the sadness of having been dragged away from his arms, also the exultation for that one dance that had no equal. Unique, unforgettable, Luis.

Their love was happy and full of surprises. A love opposed by all, by old del Fracin who in his youth had been a friend of Sacarlott's when he was still called Pidren and then after had stopped speaking to him because of Napoleon's becoming emperor. Opposed by Rosetta's brothers who had no feelings of confidence in that long, thin fellow who hurled greetings left and right. Opposed by Maria who looked upon the blacksmith's daughter as many, many levels below them and who didn't think that the raising of silkworms would have ever rendered enough to compensate for the difference.

And then, too, she's an unbeliever, la Luison declared, and that removed any remaining possibility from the del Fracin girl. Even la Gonda and la Marlattina shook their heads because of the red hair.

Only Gavriel liked this love because he felt it would not let blood, it was without tears and without reproaches, without anguish; and when he went into the fields with his brother and listened to him talk about the girl it seemed to him that his long nose, the focal point of his expression, was elaborating a story wherein happiness was possible, within hand's reach. It was born of itself, like a natural occurrence, the rain and the wind.

That's how it was for Luis, his love had no need of a future nor even of plans. He accompanied Rosetta del Fracin to pick the mulberry leaves that fattened her silkworms; he went with her to get greens for the rabbits; and they'd forget the leaves, forget the greens, so vast and unexplored was the territory in which they were adventuring and so intense the desire to know it together.

Without ever being aware of the tragedy that could be just at their shoulders: in the forgotten leaves, in the greens left to wither at the edges of the meadow. They were not afraid, not of Rosetta's brothers nor of storms, nor even of the dead that are met at dusk near cemeteries. A boundless faith in themselves flattened whatever did not concern them into an indistinct horizon, or instantly dissipated whatever could disturb them or contend their love. But this was also to have been the limit of their story, what restricted its duration and then erased any trace almost as if, turning back, they'd not be able to recognize anything, only indistinct forms from which a few trivial details remained alive: the running of a mill-stream, the soaring of a kite. Or the rhymes of the anthem in honor of Ferdinand of Austria, crowned that year in Milan.

Because the only daughter of the anarchist blacksmith has a weakness for kings and emperors: "Hail excellent son of Austria, Ferdinand Emperor...," she declaims, stretching out her arms. Difficult words for her, used to dialect, and her eyes shine as if she already could descry among ermines and carriages the brilliance of the double-headed Hapsburg eagle. Luis laughs but she continues, unperturbed, obstinate, determined to know and to see; she will not be stopped by Luis, no one will stop her and now she doesn't want him to interrupt her, she breathes the words into his mouth, bites the hand that would muffle the torrent of words. A mill-stream runs between two stands of trees, she bends over to drink, exhausted, and Luis grasps her wet fingers, sucks them between his lips until he feels them docile and warm, silence fills her lungs and only the sound of water through the grassy banks is like the shiver that comes over them. Once she lost a clog and they had to search for it when it was dark, by touch, in the grass.

Who knows if they ever made love in the full sense of the word, love that leaves one faint and satiated. Rosetta del Fracin had a great need to dream and to wait. So many bodices, so many skirts. Surely they must have come very close. Afterwards, when Luis hurt his knee and had to be immobilized for months, he thought at length of those moments in which all had been possible. He thought of how it would have happened, and what would have become of them, after. He thought, above all, of his baffling, fearless happiness. He imagined her melancholy, imagined the abandon in the gold-brown of her glance.

Afterwards, when it was already too late. When at the first frost he fell on the slippery bricks in the lane and his knee hit the ground with the full weight of his body, forming internally a sack of fluid, a fluid that for months the more it was drained, the more it re-formed. Confined to a chair, he watched from the windows to see if ever there came del Fracin's only daughter. He peered through the last, resistant leaves of the apple trees, through the dry stems of the asters planted that year for the first time. A sign, a message. And when in the morning the sun burnt off the mist and blue chunks of sky appeared, he told himself: today she'll come.

She came once only and she stopped under the vine-arbor to speak with Fantina; no one asked her in and Luis in vain tapped his fingers on the window-panes sealed by frost. She didn't once raise her head, she didn't turn her eyes upward an instant to search beyond the network of bare branches on the arbor. He saw her red hair coming out from her wool bonnet, her hands swollen and ruined from her work with the silkworms. And when he saw her go off down the lane, he broke the glass with his fist. But she was already gone and didn't hear him shout. One afternoon before Luis slipped and struck his knee, they had gone up on the hill where the Gru farm was to fly a kite. The peasants in the fields had stopped to watch that strange bird tossed by the wind, always stopped at the same point. A bird that rustled in a sky gray with clouds while the triangular flights of

migrating geese passed above it. On its wings that
bird carried the written name of del Fracin's
daughter; but the peasants couldn't see that, just as
they could not see the string that kept it tied to
earth as the night came on and the blacksmith's sons
canvassed the countryside in search of their sister.
If they had found him, that Luis, they would have
broken his bones. It was fall and Rosetta had put
her cold fingers into Luis' jacket. Above their
heads that paper bird swirled and flapped until they
forgot about it. After it was too late, the string
had gotten tangled among bushes and they had run
until they were breathless because the moon was
already risen beyond the hills and no one would
ever have been able to explain to the old blacksmith how important it was to fly a kite. Who
could have explained it to her brothers. How
marvelous.

That year, when she went to confession for
Christmas, Rosetta del Fracin never seemed to
come out of the confessional and at the end was left
by herself to say her penance while the sacristan
went about extinguishing the last candles and she
still hadn't finished. And at midnight mass, when it
was the moment of the Hallelujah her voice rose so
limpid and high that the girls' chorus fell silent.
The Provost remained with his hands open above
the chalice, stock-still, and the altar boys, aston-
ished, turned their heads. But Rosetta del Fracin's
voice was beautiful in a too earthly sense and her
Hallelujah celebrated in Christmas the light, the
warmth, the food. The people who filled the church
were poor, and they had looked upon her with
fright.

In spring, Maria took Luis to a famous doctor in Vercelli. The trip was long and tiring and when they got to the doctor, his leg was so swollen that it wasn't even possible to drain it. Luis had a high fever, he was delirious. The doctor made an incision for the full length of his knee and did two blood-lettings, then told Maria that she should keep her son awake until the knee had emptied, only thus could he be saved. All night Maria talked to Luis, she cried and told him the story of her life, and Luis stayed awake to hear it and the fluid drained right through the mattress, wetting the floor. In the morning she could see the bone through the open wound.

That trip to Vercelli was decisive. If ever Luis had had the possibility of walking as he once did, that wagon ride removed it forever. The fluid never formed again so consumed was the knee, but he was left with a thinner, lifeless leg.

It was April when he tried again to walk; wheat was beginning to push up in the fields still damp with the last snow, some cherry trees more sheltered than others were in bloom, and the scent of the elder-trees could be discerned. Leaning on Gavriel, Luis got as far as the gate. Returning he tried walking alone, he was thinking of Rosetta del Fracin and of Gru's hill, of the next kites to come. The dog nuzzled close to him and he had an instant of hesitation, then he straightened up, swayed, and finally went on. Gavriel, who was watching him, smiled. Also Maria, who so rarely smiled, seemed once again to be the Maria of before.

Whoever thought that Luis would be left disabled, did not know him well enough. Even with one leg different, he held himself as straight as before and when summer came they saw him at dances with his cap set back on his curls and the jacket that changed color in the rain.

But Rosetta del Fracin is no more, and there's no use searching out her glowing fox-color hair. Nor the blue cotton dress she made herself. No use trying to pick up her contralto voice. She's become engaged and she will be married after the grape harvest in a white gown which is already the talk of everyone. A gown given her by her brothers who went to pick out the fabric in Casale. Because Rosetta is a good girl and should be rewarded; Camurà is in love with her and doesn't even want to wait for spring, already he's fixing a house, a real house with a garden all around it and an oak tree in front of the gate. Camurà is rich, his money was made at the markets and fairs which he began to follow while still a boy pulling his cart up the hilly roadways.

Translated by Helen Barolini

MARIA
by
Dacia Maraini

When I get up in the morning to go to work Maria
is still sleeping. I slip out of bed without making
any noise so I won't wake her; taking the little pile
of clothes from the chair I go and get dressed in the
bathroom. I close the door behind me carefully
without letting it click out loud and pass through
the icy hallway. Our apartment house has no
furnace; we have some gas heaters which, however,
inconveniently warm only one section of air at a
time. So the house is divided into hot and cold
blocks that never mix with each other.

At nine o'clock I'm in the office. For the first
five minutes I'm stunned by the noise and ask
myself how I've been able to stand it up to now. I
can never get used to it. But the stupor and
paralysis last only a few minutes, the first few.
Then the noise of the machine tools beyond the
glass is changed into something tremendous: the
roar of a waterfall, broken at regular intervals by
the roll of a drum. I begin to search among the
filing cards to get the key punch started, keeping
the calculating machine within reach.

My office is a cubical of glass stuck in the
middle of an enormous room in an automobile
factory. Five other people work with me: three men
and two women. By now I've been with them more

than six years, but I can't really say I know them. I don't talk much. They chatter away, but I can't hear them: the noise drowns their voices. To make yourself heard you have to put your mouth to the ear of the listener, and I never find anything important enough to persuade me to put my mouth on the brilliantined heads of my fellow workers.

At twelve noon the siren goes off. The workers quit at once. The noise stops. At first the silence is a relief, then it becomes intolerable. I notice so many things that at first did not bother me: my eyes burning from the neon lights, my fingers numb from using the machine, the odor of sweat that floats on the tepid air.

I look up and for the first time since I came in the factory, I look at the workers. They seem happy to go out in the courtyard and eat. Some carry bottles of wine with them, others dishes of spaghetti. They pass by without seeing me. Even though the cubical is transparent and full of light, they never stop to look in. They are so used to us that it's as though we didn't exist for them.

With my eyes I follow a girl who goes by with a busy air, her black smock unbuttoned over her short skirt, her strong and muscular legs in thick red checked stockings. I look at her because her face resembles Maria's. She has prominent cheek bones, wide jaw, narrow slanting eyes, black eyebrows, a slightly mongoloid expression.

I stand up and put on my coat. I go out. When I pass by the courtyard I don't see the girl. I look at a group of women who are sitting on the ground eating by the edge of a flower bed, but I don't see her. She must be one of those who prefer the crowd and hubbub of the cafeteria.

When I get home, Maria has just gotten up. The house is a mess. The bedroom stinks of cigarettes, the bed is upside down, the bathroom a lake, the freezing kitchen full of smoke.

I begin straightening things up. Maria goes around the house in a kimono, smoking one cigarette after another. She follows behind me talking while I work.

Maria has a very nice voice. Sometimes, while I wash, clean, put the house in order, she sits on a stool in the bedroom next to the window so she can get the sun on her back, and she talks to me like I wasn't there.

Often I can't even follow her reasoning, which is deep and complicated, but I lose myself in her voice, which is clear and light and musical like a bird's.

We eat in the kitchen. Maria sits across from me and greedily eats everything I put on her plate. But she doesn't look at what she eats, because she is thinking; then her face acquires that distracted and worried look so familiar to me.

"Have you ever thought what love is between two women?"

"No."

"There must be a reason, don't you think?"

"I don't know."

"Why should I love you instead of a man? Why should I make love to you instead of a man?"

"I don't know. Because you like to."

"But why do I like to?"

"I don't know. Because you love me."

"Oh, fine, you fool. But why?"

"I really don't know."

"I think that men and women don't want to make love together any more so they won't make children. There are too many of us."

"Do you want some more cod?"

She nods yes. She brings to her mouth a big piece of cod – the most economical kind and therefore fatter and more thready – without paying any attention to its taste. I know she isn't tasting her food by her face, which chews mechanically, her eyes staring, and by her throat that hastily swallows one piece after another without stopping.

"They make me laugh when they talk of non-violence. What do we do from morning to night if not violence."

"I brought some grapes for you. Do you want them?"

"We get up in the morning and begin by killing three thousand cows."

"Cows?"

"Certainly. How many cows and little calves and sheep do you think are killed every day in a city like this one?"

"How would I know."

"And don't you suffer violence from your bosses?"

"No. They don't do anything to me."

"I don't mean physical violence. How much do they give you a month?"

"Eighty thousand lire."

"Do you know what they earn from your eighty thousand lire? At least twenty-five a month. It's all earnings robbed from you."

"What has that to do with it?"

"And when they make you stay in a cubical, in the middle of that noise, with that artificial light, for eight hours a day."

"What has that to do with it? I work and they pay me."

"Fine, stupid. You work and they rob you. That's the truth. They rob you day after day, hour after hour. And you let them rob you, you're even happy about it. Isn't that crazy?"

I start to laugh. She has such a serious, angry face it makes me laugh. I don't want to argue because soon I have to go back to work and I would like to rest a moment on the bed. But Maria doesn't want to interrupt her line of thought. She wants me to stay seated in my place, looking at her and responding, even if only occasionally.

I fix coffee. I find the coffee pot open and full of old grounds; two cigarette butts are in it.

"Why do you put your butts in the coffee pot?"

"You know what I say. You have no political conscience. You lose yourself in things, in coffee grounds, in washing powder, in codfish, in grapes, in dirty sheets. And you never think of anything that concerns everyone and not just you. You don't think of the world, of injustice. You refuse to judge. For you everything is okay. You're worse than an animal."

She makes me sad when she talks like that. Suddenly I feel tired. I don't want to do anything. I look at her hard and beautiful face, white enough to scare you.

I go into the bedroom and lie down, closing my eyes. A moment later I feel her lips touching my forehead, chin, mouth. All sadness swiftly passes.

I spend the afternoon again closed in the cubical, writing, typing, working the key punch, answering the telephone. Sometimes I raise my inflamed eyes to the glass that separates me from the rest of the department. I see bent backs, pieces of car bodies hanging from a cable in a row, black smocks in motion. The girl with the muscular legs and the mongoloid face works in another department, at a press for plastics. I see her only at noon and at closing time. She goes by the cubical without turning, swinging a bag of blue material.

One day Maria greets me with a furious face. "What's happened?" I ask her. At the same time I start straightening the bedroom. I like to move around a little after sitting for so many hours.

"You know my father is a farmer."

"Yes, you told me."

"He lives in Urbino."

"Yes."

"But you don't know what goes on in the head of a farmer who has no political conscience."

"Your father is your father. You have to love him."

"Don't be an idiot. My father is a poor farmer and should be for the revolution. Instead he is a conservative – more conservative than the men he works for. Do you understand? He is a stupid egotist who doesn't think of anything but money."

"But he is your father."

"Who cares!"

"A father is a father. And that's that."

"Fathers and mothers are our sickness. We must destroy them."

"What happened?"

"My father found out I live with you and wants to lock me up in an insane asylum."

"Why?"

"Rather than consider me 'abnormal' as he says, he prefers to pass me off as crazy."

"Have you seen him?"

"Yes, he came this morning while you were gone."

"And what did he say?"

"He said that he is ashamed of me. That in his town they say I'm abnormal, and he explained that I was crazy instead. And that he'll have me shut up in an asylum."

"But how?"

"He has a policeman friend who can help him."

"But you aren't crazy. Who would believe it?"

"My father is stubborn."

We didn't talk about it any more. Her father didn't come back to our house and after three months I thought there was no more danger.

One morning I go out to work as usual. I close myself up in the cubical. I have a series of bills to check and work all morning with the calculator. It is Saturday. At a quarter to twelve I see the workers lined up at the window of the cashier to get their pay. I wait to see the mongoloid girl, but she isn't there. Her envelope is collected by a blond girl who says she is her cousin.

At twelve I close the drawers, cover the machine with a black cloth and go home. The bus is so full that I can't get off at my stop; bodies form a wall in front of the door and before I can reach it the conductor has driven off again. And so I have to go a way on foot and when I get there it is already one o'clock.

No one is home. I think that Maria has gone to buy something. I wait until two-thirty, the time when I have to go back to the office. But Maria doesn't return.

I run to the office. I work until seven and then go home. No Maria.

Two days later I learn she has been taken to the insane asylum. I go to find her. She is more pale and worried than usual.

"Don't worry about me. I'll get out soon. Everyone knows I'm sane."

"When will you get out?"

"Soon. But what makes me mad isn't the doctors."

"What, then?"

"The patients."

"Why?"

"They are allowed to do just what they want. They don't protest, they don't argue, they don't organize. They're like you, tied to things. They live for soup, for meat, for television."

"They are sick."

"No. They are objects."

"They are sick."

"They have relinquished judgment, like you."

"When will you get out?"

"Soon."

But I can't talk to her long. The nurse comes to lock the door. Only at that moment do I realize that there is a very strong odor in that room, a wild odor, and I choke with disgust.

A week later I return to visit her. They tell me she has gone away. I'm happy and get ready to go back home when a fat blond girl comes up to tell me that Maria has killed herself.

Immediately after she bursts into a gloomy, stupid laugh. I don't know whether to believe her or not. Then, when the sister takes her by the wrist and drags her away screaming, I know that it's true.

Translated by Martha King

THE KISS IN THE SEA
by
Milena Milani

On Sunday we went to the Excelsior.

We went there late, it was past one o'clock, and it was extremely hot. I was nervous because my dress was sticking to me. Tommaso couldn't take his jacket off because in the back, high up, he had a burn in his pants. He'd leaned up against a table and come in contact with a lighted cigarette set the wrong way round in an ashtray. Now his pants had a small round hole in them and the light blue of his underwear showed through.

I had teased him: "You're in blue like a suckling babe," I had said to him, laughing.

But Tommaso's face darkened, his eyes were impenetrable. He didn't give me the satisfaction of an answer. On the motorboat that was taking us to the sea and afterwards on the tram, he was silent. I had watched Venice receding, vanishing in a light haze, and as always, the sight of her tugged at my heart.

I pretended to be cheerful.

The passing days upset me. I continually masked my emotion with gestures and words but inside me there was a strange uneasiness. I identified with the city, like her I was full of mystery while appearing transparent.

When we reached the beach, the silence between us got heavy. Tommaso undressed hurriedly, before me, and when I came out of the cabana, I didn't see him. He had already gone toward the shore.

It was the first Sunday of summer, and the very first Sunday at the beach. We never know what we'll be doing because we don't plan anything, not work, nor vacations. We live from day to day. Our companions are the provisional, the unforeseen. It could be that this is the cause of my discomfort. But Tommaso isn't even aware of it, because I have never talked about it to him.

I didn't say anything that Sunday, either. The sand was scorching hot, the water was tepid.

We took a platform boat to go off shore in search of some cool air. I was rowing and Tommaso was stretched out in front of me with his arms spread-eagle. Being blond, his skin was very fair since we hadn't been to the beach at all yet this year. His hair wasn't bleached out like other years. I wasn't tanned either but was thinking that outside on a day like today we would certainly turn dark.

So I said to Tommaso: "We'll get tanned today," but he curtly replied that it was no longer fashionable.

I rowed very slowly, following an imaginary line perpendicular to the beach, but more often I pulled harder with my right and the boat went crooked. Farther out some people were trying to water-ski and taking great falls, then a girl in a red bathing suit took off and triumphantly succeeded, going at a mad pace behind the motorboat. I didn't envy them at all and continued rowing slowly and rather distractedly. My eyes kept falling often upon

Tommaso, so relaxed, or upon the beach cabanas and the dike in the background.

It was wonderful that it was Sunday and that Tommaso had so many hours to spend with me, though he really wasn't with me because he said not one word, nor did he look at me, nor smile. He stayed stretched out without making any movement. I got bored and told him I was fed up: "You come row now," I added. "I don't feel like it anymore."

But he didn't get up and didn't even answer, so I kept heading out to sea. As we went, his wife came to mind and I thought about his children. In fury I said to myself that I would leave him. After all, the world is full of men. Tommaso already had his life all organized, that's why he was always so vague and imprecise with me. You could count the days we spent together on the fingers of one hand.

Finally I stopped, let the oars drop and quickly lay down, trying not to think anymore. At that point the boat sank lower in the water and Tommaso sat up, enraged because his back had got wet.

"Well, la-di-dah!" I said. "We're at the beach, aren't we? How could I know that the boat was already full of water?"

"You're the heavy one," he answered unkindly. "You must weigh a ton."

"And you must weigh two," I answered back. "You are truly obese."

It wasn't true at all. Tommaso is not fat, and I don't weigh a ton. We were saying that just to hurt each other. In fact, this time Tommaso was wounded and immediately became nicer.

"Do you really mean it?" he asked.

Since I was smiling ironically, he kept on: "Maybe I really am fat? I weighed myself a few days ago and I thought I'd lost."

"Oh, no," I replied. "You haven't lost weight at all. Look." I pointed to the folds on his stomach. Then, wickedly, I kept on: "You eat too much at home. Who knows what food they prepare for you."

He didn't get the insinuation. Instead he replied: "You are in the same shape I'm in. Inevitably, since all we do is sit."

So I took a deep breath and tightened my stomach muscles. My abdomen went flat. I held it for a few seconds then relaxed. Right afterwards I went for a dip, swimming slowly around the boat, enjoying the coolness of the water on my skin. Off shore, the water wasn't hot like it was near the beach and it really cooled you off. It was limpid and a pale green color.

"Come in for a swim," I exclaimed. "It's wonderful."

"I don't feel like it," said Tommaso, but he turned around to watch me swim.

I was now thinking about the mess we'd gotten ourselves into. He's in a double bind, to his family and to me. Any decisions were far off in the future so we both avoided broaching the subject. I looked at the sky for a moment and hoped that help might come to me from those high regions.

Everything was still – the air, the heat, life itself and even time passing. So I took a mouthful of water and moved up to the boat. I squirted the water on Tommaso and he was extremely annoyed, yelling at me to cut out the pranks. I'd become rather light-hearted by now and had no intention of stopping. I squirted him again and he was forced to dive in.

Wisely I'd taken my distance, fearing his reaction and that game he likes where he puts a hand on my head and pushes me under to drink salt water. When I come up all dazed, he pushes me under again and again, until I can't take anymore and I promise not to play any more tricks on him. But this time Tommaso doesn't come after me in the water nor does he try to punish me. Turning on his side, he heads out with a kind of old-fashioned stroke.

His escape stirred my affection for him. I thought how he was a man and I still a girl. There were years of difference between us. Could Tommaso leave everything in order to be with me? And did I have the right to ask him to do that? Or was I to wait until he made the decision on his own? I abandoned those thoughts and hollered: "Hey, Tommaso! Don't go too far out. It's dangerous."

He didn't reply, nor did he look back, so I tried to swim out to him. In that instant I felt like his slave. But when I finally got close, I grabbed one of his feet and squeezed hard. Tommaso gave a scream of rage and I laughed till water filled my mouth.

"Listen, Tommaso," I said in a conciliatory tone. "Today is Sunday and we're at the beach. Let's not fight over these dumb things."

"Dumb things? You hurt my foot!"

"I hurt you on purpose because you were going away and didn't answer when I called you."

"I didn't hear you."

"There, you see, you're the same old liar. How could you not hear if I was shouting?" And I was thinking of the lies men tell, the daily falsehoods of us all, men and women, involved in love affairs.

"What were you shouting?" he asked, fully obedient to the pre-established ritual.

"I was shouting that it was dangerous, because I was afraid," I answered in my role as victim and, so saying, I moved closer to him. I put my arms around his neck, consigned myself to my sweet executioner.

"You'll sink me," objected Tommaso. "Do you want me to drown?"

"Certainly not," I said and put my salty mouth to his. Tommaso didn't move so I kissed him again.

Translated by Barbara Dow Nucci

MY MOTHER WORE PINK

by

Milena Milani

My mother, dressed in pink, was sitting close to me in the water-taxi. Out of the corner of my eye, so as not to upset her, I watched her. I observed her profile, her white-gloved hands resting on her knees. Her delicate skin, typical of blondes, had acquired a uniform gold tone, a few freckles sprinkled here and there which added to her prettiness.

Her face, under the brim of the rough straw hat, stayed turned to one side. Even without wanting to, I was guessing the thoughts that passed through her mind.

People got on and off at the various stops, and the boat headed for the open sea, gradually speeding up. From the open door came the wind and even the smell of the sea.

My mother was quiet and, turning her profile toward me slightly, she sometimes hinted at a smile, her lip turning up in a wrinkle to the left. Then she quickly regained her outward appearance of impassivity.

I was taken up with my usual nervousness, which manifests itself first in something precise and perceptible, right down in my throat or in my stomach. It's a kind of secret gnawing, which I can do nothing about. I almost cannot think since my brain goes fossilized on one position.

This time the position was my mother, her body next to mine.

She wasn't aware of my distress, if distress in me is ever visible (many times I've been told that I hide my thoughts very well). She was almost provoking me with her very impassivity. I'd even say she was irritating me.

She was completely in the dark about what I was feeling. She wasn't trying at all to understand. Quite the opposite, she was almost completely absorbed in obstinately watching the glass door nearby. I knew very well that by now her eyes had so observed it that every last detail of it had been assimilated. That door didn't interest me one bit.

All the same, in solidarity, I began to look at it and I noticed that it was made of light wood, almost yellow, recently polished. The glass panes were punctuated with black spots here and there.

"They haven't washed them," I was forced to say and I said these words clearly enough that my mother answered: "It's the flies."

"In this season?" I continued.

"I guess there are some around here," replied my mother. In truth she wasn't very convinced because we have lived around here for a long time.

I didn't say anything else nor did my mother.

Our trip seemed to reabsorb the attention of us both, but I don't remember now exactly what we looked at. The water was violently thrust aside by the bow and a little of it fell on us through the open window. Just a few drops and they wet my dress. Not even my nervous gesture disturbed my mother.

She only said, without getting upset: "It was just a little water."

Right afterwards, though, her mouth contracted and her hands in their white gloves moved about, cutting the air.

"May I ask why you are moving about so?" I asked. But she didn't give me any answer and this time her hands went back to her knees and stayed there forsakenly.

I began to stare at them and I deliberately said to myself: "Move you hands, I order you to move your hands." Issuing a command like that gave me a strange pleasure.

I worked this form of will in vain, however. After looking at me with sadness in her eyes, almost as if she understood what I was saying, she remained motionless, and I became sorrowful with her.

Translated by Barbara Dow Nucci

ICE CREAM
by
Milena Milani

There were days when I would buy myself a half-pint of ice cream and I couldn't wait to get home so I could eat it. I would always choose strawberry and lemon, deceiving myself that they weren't fattening since it was fruit. The flavors I liked very much – cream, cocoa, vanilla – I deliberately passed up after looking at them one last time and reading the ingredients, the warnings and all the rest on the packaging.

When I fished greedily around in the big freezer compartments where the containers of ice cream were (there were many different brands and even pint-size cartons), the frost, which formed around them in tiny white slivers and often contracted into whimsical ornaments, became a bizarre fire which shot up to my heart. Absurdly I flamed up like an adolescent and furtively looked around me to see if anyone had noticed.

People were passing by and lingering in the vast supermarket. There were many foreigners, mostly Germans, elderly women with short white socks in plastic sandals, skirts gathered at the waist, stiff hair. I hated those tourists, they made me furious. They were strong with evident muscles, large hands. The men wore colored and patterned bermuda shorts, jerseys over chests whose pectorals were like those of horses or draught mules who had reached the Dolomites.

I was, in fact, in the mountains, and they invaded the valley, all over the place with those guttural voices which sometimes drove me crazy with rage. I would have thrown them into their cars and forced them to leave quickly. But then I read the newspapers and watched TV and I said to myself that one must tolerate them.

The balance of payments needed their currency, those bank notes, those coins. I, too, dealt in currency. I paid money to buy that ice cream, not a great sum, mind you. For one thousand eight hundred lire I took home those two hundred and fifty grams of afternoon ardor.

I went out around six pm on certain dark days when the desire for the carton (that round box of cardboard with its cover that I removed hurriedly, licking the inside of it so as to not leave one bit of that burning cold) made me absurdly nervous and restless. I moved fast along the street, almost running and without looking at anyone. From the house to the supermarket I went through Concordia Park, taking a private road with a sign that said "no trespassing" but that no one obeyed.

As I left my condominium, my eyes rested for a moment, almost against my will, on a large green meadow there to the left, at the bottom of which there were many trees. Here and there, in the shade or sun, were lawn chairs, cots with foam rubber mattresses, slides for children, and swings. I could glimpse semi-nude bodies, I could hear laughter and voices, but it was as if in a dream, because I was propelled by a strange anxiety. I felt even sick, I was losing my breath. I wanted the ice cream, as I would have wanted a man, to devour. Afterwards my mouth was left bitter, with a taste of ashes.

Let's take things in order. It was a Thursday of this year, of this summer. The slogans and the publicity continued to tell us to keep our regular partner, because it is dangerous to move out from the couple circuit, to look elsewhere. I was on my own, in the company of an old castrated cat who sat like an idol on the terrace and who thought only of eating when he came back into the apartment. After, he would go to sleep and not consider me at all. If I spoke to him, he'd open one eye, turn over and go back to sleep.

Food was the bond between the cat and me. How well I understood his cravings, since I had them too. At times I would have cruelly beaten him, tortured him, but instead I rushed out and went to the freezer compartments of the supermarket where the ice cream was in ordered stacks, shiny with the frost that decorated them. I extricated my carton from the others, already tasting with pleasure that fleeting flavor, its pink and white sweetness. I pronounced to myself those two colors, sounding out consonants and vowels, and next to me, behold, a nordic giant putting his hands there in the middle, touching the cartons and my bare arms.

He was blond with blue eyes, his skin fair, untanned by the sun, and the fact that he was so child-like pleased me. He laughed and looked at me provocatively. Or did I misinterpret his simplicity, inventing meanings that weren't there? He, too, had taken a carton of ice cream and he followed me to the check-out. While I was paying, he handed the cashier the money for his purchase and left with me, all with the skill of a juggler.

Though tall and big, he moved gracefully all the same. Suddenly a curious warmth invaded my body as if it were already in contact with his. *"Schon,"* he said, and I wasn't sure what he was referring to. I felt that all was beautiful around us, the mountains, the greenery, life, every step I took, the timelessness of that Thursday, the noise of a helicopter above us. I looked up trying to catch sight of it but it was hidden from view by the trees. The drone of its motor faded and the two of us (no longer I alone but I with the giant) went up the usual Concordia route, each carrying his and her respective ice cream package.

It was comical, though not to me, but I felt very weak, devoid of strength, just the way Eve walked before they threw her out of Paradise. Long hair over her bare shoulders, that supple body of first woman of the world, progenitrix of a degenerate species, of horrible fat women, devourers of ice cream, with swollen greedy mouths and anteater tongues.

Who knows why I envisioned so distinctly that toothless mammal like one I'd seen in a magazine a few days ago. It came to mind with its long snout and its threadlike, sticky tongue which it thrusts into antholes. I had a feeling of disgust, my mouth filled with saliva, I felt like vomiting. I stopped and screamed.

The giant with the blue eyes, white of skin, blond of hair, suddenly changed. He was rapidly transformed – massive, vulgar, with little red veins on his cheeks, evident wrinkles, balding, his fingernails bordered in black, and those ridiculous short pants showing calves, repulsive thighs. An undershirt beneath his short-sleeved shirt, even the plastic sandals and socks like his countrymen.

His eyes, his glance. Could perhaps the enchantment stay fixed in the pupils and from there spread with tenderness, the very thing every creature unconsciously desires, waits for, wants for himself? On beds in summertime, sweating together, loving each other, that is *schon*, even if your partner is occasional, even if he's unfamiliar, unknown. One needs to begin an adventure in order to break the solitude, to stop eating ice cream, to communicate.

I looked at him, terrorized because even his eyes were changing. Smaller they were, tired, insipid, without spark or light. They did not express one fleeting thought, feeling or desire. A dead fish with those eyes.

And now I was running, because my ice cream was melting. I wanted to halt its dissolution.

Translated by Barbara Dow Nucci

RITA'S TRIP
by
Marina Mizzau

Until it happened, Rita would never have believed that it could happen, that there would have been a moment when she would have wanted to do something without Giulio. At most, at various times she had wanted to want to do it, to put some distance between them, out of vindictiveness, or out of helplessness, from exasperation or desperation, or maybe also from a vague yearning for freedom; but it was always a matter of an abstract desire, too easily perishable, that dissolved at the mere sound of a doorbell.

Rita used to wait for Giulio's arrival with a book in hand, but if Giulio was late she couldn't go on reading. Rita closed the book, or whatever else she might have had open when Giulio arrived. Rita said, "They've said that this weekend will be sunny," and she waited for Giulio to suggest going to the beach; but she herself could never suggest it directly, because she was too afraid that Giulio might say no, and this wouldn't have had to do just with going to the beach. Rita didn't express desires. She always tried instead to anticipate Giulio's, including his desire that she should not make him see that she wanted him too much.

Rita didn't have friends. Not because Giulio prevented her; rather, he urged her to have them.

But to find herself in the predicament of having to give up spending time with Giulio on account of having taken on another obligation, since that would have left him unexpectedly free, was an idea that filled her with intolerable anxiety. She had nevertheless decided, after some wavering, that surrendering him once and for all cost less than the attrition and piecemeal loss of struggling to keep him, cost less than victories that made her much more unhappy than did defeats.

After all, Rita did love Giulio, she lived for Giulio, she waited for Giulio, she cross-examined herself on the subject of Giulio, on her mood and her love, and she thought too that Giulio might not like all this love and availability, but she couldn't do otherwise.

Rita had an uninteresting job that hardly distracted her from thinking about Giulio. It happened though that she was asked to go to New York on business, replacing a co-worker – a ten-day separation from Giulio not wanted by him, as usual, but initiated by her. Rita's first reaction was to think that it was impossible: the second was dismay because she found that it was indeed possible.

Rita had to decide. She wasn't obliged to go, but her boss wanted her to. Unexpectedly one evening – she was waiting for Giulio, who was late as usual – she realized that she herself wanted to go. She felt guilty and thought that she was bound to lose Giulio: she couldn't get over her fixation, her wretched worry over Giulio, and over Giulio's absences, or square it with an absence of her own.

Then there were many other phases: excitement, fear, denial, euphoria, fear again, anxiety, indifference. Finally, without joy, but with stoic determination, she told herself that she had to make this gesture of autonomy, to prove the point to Giulio. Rita decided that she had to go.

A week or so later, as the date of her departure drew near, she wasn't quite sure whether she was glad to be going to New York, or to have been able to decide to go, and so to leave Giulio. She quit asking herself about it when she found she was pleasurably involved in anticipating what she might do in New York, her thoughts for the first time far removed from Giulio.

It was then that Giulio said to her: "I'd like to see New York, I've never been there; I think I could go with you."

Rita was dumbfounded not to feel instantly overjoyed. Perhaps it was panic at seeing a structure miraculously stable despite the imbalance of its parts, or perhaps stable just because of that imbalance, sway; or it might have been the disorientation of seeing a project involving long-term change cancelled out by a change that was too abrupt, or it might have been – who knows? – a heady sense of freedom squelched just as it was barely beginning to take shape. In any case the effect of Giulio's proposal at first provoked in Rita only bewilderment.

Then, almost out of guilt for this first reaction, Rita began to consider the matter in another light. At once the somewhat heroic fantasy of herself alone in New York was replaced by a divergently seductive one of herself in New York with Giulio.

Rita now thinks about the ten days in New York with Giulio, and already she regrets the time that she'll have to devote to work and to being apart from him. If not for this it would really be a great carefree holiday. Now she is happy over this prospect that has come her way without even having to deal with her own desire. That at its inception the project of the trip was hers alone, she has already forgotten. She has forgotten the euphoria that her choice of going it alone had brought her.

A few days before the date set for departure, Giulio says to her: "You know, I've reconsidered, I'm not going to New York. I think it's better if you go alone; it'll do you good to be away from me for a while, to do something completely on your own."

Rita will leave tomorrow for New York and she searches in vain for some feeling. She no longer expects anything – not from the trip nor from the return, and not much from her life, either.

Translated by Blossom S. Kirschenbaum

THE SALT FOR BOILING WATER
by
Marina Mizzau

"Salt for cooking spaghetti goes in when the water's cold," one of the two women was saying, the not-so-young one.

From her post the cashier heard everything that took place at the tables. Not that she particularly cared to hear, but she could hardly help it. The restaurant was small and at least two of the tables were quite close to the cashier's booth, which moreover was almost hidden by a screen; not hidden to the degree that the patrons might fail to know of her presence, but enough so that they might forget they knew and might not realize they were being overheard. She therefore could hardly help hearing, and this was her misfortune, for she disliked arguments, and besides, after so many experiences, she could no longer even try to persuade herself that no, there was nothing beyond the commonplaces, and once those people had gone away from there, not a trace of them would remain.

That evening the nearest table was occupied by three individuals, two women and a man.

"No, it goes in when the water is about to boil, that way it speeds up the boiling," replied the younger woman, rather satisfied, it seemed, to contribute to the conversation, even if by contradicting. The cashier hoped that would end it, and perhaps this time around she really would be able to dismiss what she had heard. But the truce was quite brief.

"Why no, that doesn't speed it up, just the opposite, that slows it down," replied the other woman, and at this point it could be inferred that other motives were at stake beyond keeping up the conversation.

"But yes, that speeds it up, right she is," said the man, with the tone of confirming a truth always known but never uttered, and as though the moment had only now arrived to say it.

The not-so-young woman eyed the man with suspicion, and so that he should get the point of the suspicion, she underscored it with a fluttery laugh. "But you know you've always put it in when the water's cold," she said.

"I? Well, yes, could be, I don't recall." There is a touch of complaisance in the man's voice, as though to indicate the irrelevance of facts before universals, or as though he were already bored with the discussion and wanted to end it. "However," he adds, "right she is; salt put into hot water speeds up the boiling."

"It speeds it up if it's already boiling, but it doesn't make it boil if it's not boiling," says the not-so-young woman, underscoring the difference with a patiently didactic tone, like someone who pretends to believe she has not made herself clear, rather than admit the unpardonable indignity that the other person really meant what he said.

Obviously the younger woman does not take advantage of the way out. "Believe me, salt speeds up the boiling," she says, in a tone equally calm, as if she had to convince a stubborn little girl, or as if in her turn she wanted to pretend not to believe in the sincerity of the other woman's conviction.

"We, in fact, always put the salt in cold water." The voice of the not-so-young woman now has a nuance of challenge. She says, "we" accompanying the fusion of the first-person-plural pronoun with a nod of her head in his direction, and she says it without looking at him, looking rather at the other woman. She doesn't ask his agreement; she asks the other woman to take note of the facts of the matter.

"All right, fine, as you please," says the younger woman. "As you both please," she amends. But she has winked at him. Certainly she has done that. The other woman, at least, knows that she has done that, even if she isn't looking at him.

It was not an unfounded suspicion, then. Now in fact it's clear that what she was afraid of has happened. Her claim of a united front has done nothing else than provoke a catastrophic alliance. Two currents of purpose, opposed to her own, are flowing in the same direction, are seeking each other out, are joining, are making a barrier against her. They have agreed to give in for now. But they are not quits, let her not have delusions, poor naive girl, does she really think that he thinks the salt goes in when the water is about to boil? Hasn't she figured out that he has only taken advantage of the situation?

But moreover, even if it's so, if he is in bad faith, what advantage can be gained from it?

"God, that tableful of students. Listen to the filth they're talking. That collegiate rowdiness is really making a comeback." The man is evidently trying to find a neutral zone, a ground on which a united front might be inevitable. Finger-pointing:

that's the thing that's easiest. But it's too easy. She, the not-so-young woman, cannot accept it. "Why not?" she says. "After all, they're having a good time. They don't do any harm." She has to see how far she can get, offer herself as a target. "What's getting into you?" says the younger woman. "This wave of nostalgia has swept you back into the Fifties."

"Lay off," says the man nervously, "don't you see she's joking?" An offer of escape, or a threatening order to retreat; whichever one it may be, she, the not-so-young woman, cannot accept it.

"Just so," she says, "I'm joking; like them, the students, and they're doing just fine."

Evidently the man thinks this is the chance to follow her, whichever direction she may be going. "There's nothing wrong in having a good time," he announces, as though on stage. Thus all possibilities are open, including the one that she may accept the joke, recognize it and make one of her own, even that she may, on this basis of impartial exchange of irony and self-irony, make a united front between the two of them. Especially if the other, the younger woman, does not fall into line, as in fact occurs.

"But you two are crazy," she says, "it's anything but a longing for those days."

The not-so-young woman holds her tongue. Evidently she's unsure. Should she pick up on the proposed alliance he is offering? Declare that yes, she was joking. Stop taking sides, encompass the other woman too in the reconstituted united front. Oh god, if she were to do it. It would be enough were she just to laugh.

In fact, she laughs. But what laugh is it? Bitter, indulgent, parental, sarcastic?

No, the cashier fails to understand, and can't let it go at that. They can't leave her this way, she must understand, they must understand that she must understand.

By now they have asked for the check and are getting up. They leave. As always, nothing has been settled.

It would be nice, just this evening, not to hear any more and not to know any more.

But already the silence that has taken over at the first table allows the voices from the second one to emerge. They are two couples.

"Since when do you put cheese in your soup?" says one of the men.

"Why? I like it," replies one of the women.

"Matter of fact, it's good that way," agrees the other man.

"But you never put it in," the other woman says.

Translated by Blossom S. Kirschenbaum

BERLIN ANGEL
by
Giuliana Morandini

She walked past as she had done so many times before. Her hands were rather cold. As usual she kept them in her pockets, holding the passport tightly in her right hand to feel safer; she might get lost just like that, by magic, under an evil spell.

The young soldier looked her over while pretending he was engaged in something else; her features seemed to puzzle him.

Erika took the passport and permit out of her pocket and raised them fan-like before her cold face. The soldier took them and stepped back inside; she saw him light a cigarette behind the window pane.

Crossing a border always gave her a strange feeling. As a child she felt somehow thrilled when she was tossed about from one country to another. She walked across the border, looking for the vague difference between one side and the other. After all, she could turn back at the very last minute or keep going: this free choice appealed to her.

In these days to pass the frontier meant to experience how deeply the city was affected by the division, a wound that didn't heal.

In the sunshine the broken window panes of empty houses mirrored deserted rooms. Walled-up windows demanded freedom through the crevices that some roots of shrubs had opened in the cracked bricks.

A child-faced sentinel was standing still by the box; he was holding a machine gun bigger than himself, as they say. The weapon hung down across his chest and seemed to hamper his movements; his arms were short. His superiors hadn't taken into consideration the fact that killing requires skill and speed; they were satisfied with determination to strike, to let no one go through.

The boy soldier was looking at her. He knew that with the permit she would safely go ahead into the neutral zone. The other soldier outside the hut was checking and stamping the papers.

A sign revealed that there had been a hotel here once; it was still there, though it wasn't recognizable as one any longer. It was a dead place, and yet offices lived inside it, rooms received and sent news, papers and files piled up. Soldiers went in and out – they were so young that none of them stopped to think what sort of building it had once been.

A few small plants tried to grow in between two stones by a window roughly walled up with heaped bricks and stones. The stones had been used to support a machine gun, and the house in front of it, which belonged to the other side, was pockmarked from the bursts: a face incurable from the smallpox caught when young, when the tissue is delicate and the infection leaves larger pits. The contaminated skin made the holes appear in relief. The sun was laying some reflections carefully on the ravaged surface and eating away its outline, while seeking the most visible parts and pausing on the edges where the virus had carved its mark. Rain had made

117

the sound parts of the face flabby – the eyelids, which, by a special disposition of nature, were left untouched by the disease. The eyes under them were clearer, like those of sick people before they die, when they want to see a bit more before leaving life; they gaze at the way they will be going; perhaps someone behind their eyelids points it out to them. Who knows!

Berlin is a non-stop construction site. A meaningless building race to decide who builds first and who does it higher and better.

Budapesterstrasse is nothing like it used to be. Erika hated it at once. Years have gone by since the street was built, and the trees of nearby Tiergarten still claim space for their roots. After the war dust is all that is left of the garden the Elector wanted back in the eighteenth century; and yet, the plants have avenged themselves by mixing pollen and seeds in the air and by continuing to grow in the ancient design. Sometimes excavators dig up centuries-old roots clinging to one another like human bodies.

When Erika passed by at midday there was already no through traffic. Cars were being diverted and people had stopped to watch others at work, as in the old days. It had happened just then, during the midday break. The huge drill had ceased to thrust its woodworm-like tool into the ground, and the crane was hanging halfway up in the air like an elephant's trunk. A small boy had seen it first. Then, in a few minutes a youthful crowd had rushed there from the hotels in the skyscrapers, the doorways of the air-travel agencies, the automobile showrooms, the nearby Europa Center. At first people thought of a big accident, then of something funny: the zoo was close by and maybe one of the animals had come down toward the public without waiting for visitors to be attracted by the image carved in the pink stones of the entrance. But it was only the ancient roots, dark and twisted, as though the remains of Roman legions. "It's an old story that roots look like bodies," somebody said. "It's nothing strange." The crane kept silent, motionless in the air.

The young people in jeans have gone back to the Europa Center; they tarry in front of the water clock and its glass pipe. Colored liquids flow through them marking a rhythm.

The man began to tell a story long impressed in his memory, an old tale in the dead of the evening.

"So our love began, on a day like many, in a season like any other. Seasons follow each other in a natural pattern, outside ourselves and our disorder. It was a month like any other. It was cool and raining. A love was born in a corner of wounded Europe. How can I describe Sophie and the way she loved? There was no one like her, she was unique. I didn't care about her lunacy... It might show up when her clear eyes darkened, and fear haunted her forehead, lining it with shadows. Her mouth went livid and phantoms shook her body. Then I could love her, make love to her as to no other woman. She embraced me tenderly, and when she held me tighter, I knew a fit was about to come. Still, could I help getting into her and touching her white body, her swelling breasts? I didn't have to love her insane spells, I had to stay by her and wait for her orgasms to melt like snow. Everything was

119

natural in her, a sweet fluid which lingers on the skin long after it is washed away. Sophie came to me, entered the room, and I no longer knew what went on outside. I listened to her voice, the words were like drops of an elixir deposited in my memory. I touched her hair and felt grass rustling on her skin; I caressed her neck and perceived her veins pulsing like a newly-hatched bird, unable to live without a warm nest. I half closed her eyelids and brushed the wings of swallows....

"She had the strength of an angel, a golden quiver, and then icy cold. You know, she told me, an angel hindered Jacob from climbing the ladder, led Joseph and Peter beyond narrow destiny; it was an angel, too, who flew head-down over hosts and scattered them. Yes, she knew it, angels rise from the soul, and she would say over and over, their rustling wings suspend all memory.

"She showed me an angel. It stood at the head of a bridge over the Elbe, as though set apart from a bygone migration. You see, she whispered, the water has offered the marble the majestic flow of its stream and the fear of its whirlpool....

"Sophie used to talk to the angel," he went on and his voice sounded like fluttering wings. "Angels herald messages and sometimes their sign chills, it can't be avoided... Yes, if only you knew how Sophie stared at the water... It was an afternoon in spring, not long before, or a few days earlier, I don't know: this is maybe the only detail I can't remember so well. No," he added, while touching his wrists and knee joints, "a few days earlier, now I remember, it's just as if it were here and now."

"Sophie said," he added almost cooly, "'The river will turn into blood.' When she said these words, I had the feeling I could make love to her no more, get into her. I don't know why, but I suddenly realized her mind would never trace its way back to me, not even on reaching orgasm. 'What did you say, Sophie?' I asked, and that was one of the few times I questioned her, as a child speaks to a dumb toy. Her face was leaning against the window pane, only her forehead...her high and slightly curved forehead with bluish shades on her right temple. Again the light quiver of an angel vibrated in her, his crystal prophecy resounded. 'Leonard,' she called to me, 'look over there at the river, our people will be there, they will cling to one another just like the clothes on the angel we love so much. The wind will roll them over, one over the other; their mouths will have no lips, they will be united in the abyss.'

"Sophie's madness had seen, her mind was shaping, something certain. Soon the angel's voice would change into a blade that would come down as on the Assyrian camp before Jerusalem's walls; sleep would turn into fire and then cold and silence."

Translated by Margherita Piva

THE MIRRORS
by
Elsa Morante

Aracoeli. In the first years of our cohabitation, this name of hers, obviously, had a completely natural sound to me. But when we were taken, she and I, out into the world, I became aware that it set her apart from the other women in the city. In fact, the women of our acquaintance were called Anna, Paola, or Luisa, or in some cases Raimonda, Patrizia, Perla, or Camilla. "Aracoeli!" the ladies would cry. "What a lovely name! What a strange name!"

I learned later that in Spain it is common to baptize girls with such names, even Latin ones, from the church or from the liturgy. Nevertheless, gradually, as I grew up, that name Aracoeli became stamped in my memory as a sign of distinction, a unique title: in which my mother remains separate and enclosed, as in a heavy tortile frame painted with gold.

Perhaps this image of a frame comes to me from the mirror that did actually exist in our first, clandestine room, whence it then followed us into our new, legitimate house in the Heights. And there it stayed, in my parents' bedroom, large and conspicuous in the center of the wall, until our financial collapse. After that I don't know where it ended up, whether it was handed on to a relative or sold off with the rest of our furniture to some antique dealer or junk man. In all likelihood, however, it still exists, and survives the family that has vanished.

Its face was shiny and of recent manufacture; but the frame, old and fading in its gilt, was of a majestic seventeenth-century style. That style contrasted with the very modern (then called *rational*) tone that prevailed in our house; and in fact, like the French carpet at its feet, and like a few other pieces scattered here and there, it had come, through Raimonda, from my paternal grandparents in Turin.

According to some necromancers, mirrors are bottomless chasms, which swallow, but never devour, the lights of the past (and perhaps also of the future). Now, the very first posthumous view of myself, which serves as background for all of my years, appears to my memory (or perhaps pseudo-memory?) not directly, but reflected in that mirror, and enclosed by the well-known frame. Is it possible that it remained fixed there, in the subaqueous worlds of the mirror, to be returned to me today, its atoms reassembled, from the void? They say, in fact, that our recollections cannot go farther back than our second or third year; but that intact and almost immobile scene returns to me from an earlier time.

In it you see, seated on a little armchair of yellow-gold plush (already known to me, familiar) a woman with an infant nursing at her breast. She is resting a bare foot on the bed; and on the floor, on the French carpet, there is an overturned slipper. I cannot clearly make out her dress (a long dressing gown, of a fuchsia color), but I recognize her way of opening its fastenings over her bosom, taking care to expose barely the tip of her breast, with a downright comical modesty: a mother who is modest even in front of her own puppy. We are, in

fact, alone, the two of us, in the bedroom; and I am
that infant with the little black head, who every so
often raises his eyes to her.

There. At this moment the mirror vanishes, with
its frame. Now from that mirrored sight, which
seemed painted, there approach me, growing in
physical concreteness, the intimate details, as if the
me of today had again the very pupils of that
ecstatic little being clinging to the breast. Can
this be one of my apocryphal memories? In its
constant working, the restless machine of my brain
is capable of manufacturing for me visionary recon-
structions – at times as remote and fictitious as a
fata morgana, and at times so close and possessive
that I am incarnate in them. It happens, in any case,
that some apocryphal memories later prove more
true than the truth.

And this is such a one. From the half-closed
eyelids of the me of that time I see again her breast,
bared and white, with its little blue veins and,
around the nipple, a little halo of orange-pink
color. The breast is round, not big but swollen; and
often my little pawing hands seek it as I suck on it,
encountering her hand which holds it out, revealing
and covering it at the same time. Her hand, like her
neck and face – later, with time, they paled –
compared with the breast is of a much darker hue,
and is short and stubby, the nails also stubby in
their almost rectangular form. From some girlhood
wound, the knuckles of the little finger and the ring
finger have remained swollen and slightly
misshapen.

Her milk has a sweetish taste, tepid, like that of
the tropical coconut just plucked from the palm.
Every now and then, my enamored eyes are raised to
thank her face, which bends, enamored, toward me,
among the black, uneven bunches of curls that touch

her shoulders (she never wanted to cut them; it was one of her disobediences).

Her forehead is covered with curls down to her eyebrows. When she brushes her hair from her face, baring her brow, she acquires a different physiognomy, of strange intelligence and unaware, congenital melancholy. Otherwise, hers is the intact physiognomy of nature: between trust and defense, curiosity and peevishness. In her blood, all the same, there vibrates continually a delight, in the simple fact of being born.

"Eyes like a starry night" seems a literary phrase. But I could think of no other way to describe her eyes. Their irises are black, and as I remember it, this black expands beyond the iris, in a tremor of tiny drops or glints. The eyes are big, somewhat oblong, the lower lid heavy, as in certain statues. The thick brows (only later would she learn to thin them with a razor) meet on her forehead, making a circumflex accent, giving her at times, when she looks down, a stern expression, dark and almost surly. The nose is well-shaped and straight, not whimsical. The outline of the face is a full oval, and the cheeks are still a bit plump, like a child's.

Even today I think that it would be difficult for nature, in all its variety, to produce a more beautiful face. And yet, if I hammer with special insistence at my memory – shouting to myself a uniqueness that cannot be repeated – there are certain irregularities and flaws in that face: the little scar from a burn on the chin; the too-small teeth, somewhat separated; the lower lip that juts below the upper, giving her, when serious, a suspended or interrogative air, and when smiling, a helpless or dazed quality. And similarly, of her body in those days, the first aspects revived for me, with irreparable affection, are a certain asymmetry, or clumsiness, even certain defects, not perceived by me at that time: the head perhaps too big for her thin shoulders; the stocky, rural legs, with their overdeveloped calves, in contrast with the still-frail arms and body; a certain awkwardness in her walk (especially when she practiced wearing high heels); and the short, broad feet, the toes uneven and a bit twisted, the toenails ill-formed. Even after she had borne me, her body remained almost virginal, with certain girlish angularities and the suspicious, gawky movements of an animal taken from its habitat.

And then I look myself in the eyes. We rarely look into our own eyes, and apparently in some cases this amounts to an extreme exercise. They say that, plunging into our own eyes in the mirror – with crucial attention and at the same time with abandonment – we can discern in the depth of the pupil the ultimate Other, indeed the one and true Oneself, the center of every existence and of ours, in short that point that should bear the name God. Instead, in the watery puddle of my eyes I glimpse nothing but the little diluted (as if shipwrecked) shadow of that usual backward *niño* who vegetates, isolated, inside me. Unchanging, with his claim to love by now obsolete and useless, but obdurate to the point of indecency.

El niñomadrero. The mama's-boy fairy tale is stagnant, typical retrieval of a psychoanalytic session, or subject of an edifying pop song. Once upon a time there was a mirror where, looking at myself, I could fall in love with myself; it was your eyes, Aracoeli, that crowned me king of beauty in their little bewitched pools. And this was the mirage that you fabricated for me at the beginning, projecting it on all my future Saharas, beyond your horrors and your death. Your body has dissolved, with no eyes now or milk or menstruation or saliva. It has been rejected by space, is nothing but a base raving; whereas I survive, white-haired Narcissus who will not die, misled by your mirages. Surely it was you who forbade me girls as an adult, jealous of them because they were fresh and beautiful, while you were no more than a livid ghost. And you instilled in me your envy and voluptuousness, until I was made your cheap performer. You condemned me to mime your motherly role, flinging me into the pursuit of one beardless Narcissus after another, following the usual mirage of your betrayed little boy, what I had been. And so, I was surprised to find myself dazed, playing the doll, in imitation of you (had I not been your doll?); and poisoned forever by your milk, I humiliated myself in maniacal imploration, I prostrated myself, I moaned. Jester, thanks to your ghostly game, to the little nighttime toughs of the streets, subject to their mockery, disgust, blackmail, blows, and lynching. If you had at least given birth to me among them, one of their class. Instead you made me a bourgeois, which today means lackey.

And now, where are you taking me? Perhaps El Almendral doesn't exist. It is one of your conspiracies to set me on false trails, after having deceived me as a child. Now you have slipped away like a thief; and I find myself here, alone and naked, before this *ropero de luz – espejo de cuerpo entero,* which quite unceremoniously flings into my face my real form. And who would not be disgusted by this monkey, when I disgust myself first of all?

Every creature on earth offers himself. Pathetic, ingenuous, he offers himself: "I am born! Here I

am! with this face, this body, and this smell. Do I
appeal to you? Do you want me?" From Napoleon
to Lenin and Stalin, to the last streetwalker, to the
mongoloid child, to Greta Garbo and Picasso and
the stray dog, this in reality is the one perpetual
question of every living being to the other living
beings: "Do I seem beautiful to you? I, who to *her*
seemed the most beautiful?" And each one then
takes to displaying his own beauties; whence our
desperate vanities are explained: The publicity
ravings of starlets, and the grimaces of generalis-
simos, and powers, and finance, and kamikazes and
mountain-climbers and tightrope-walkers; and every
achievement, every record ("For *her* I was the most
beautiful of all"). Orphans, never weaned, all
living creatures suggest themselves, like people of
the street, at another's signal of love. A crown or a
title or applause or a curse or alms or a piece of
trade. You pay me, and so you accept my body.
You kill me, and so you damn yourself for me.

Always for the same demand, or boast, or claim,
we hand ourselves over to the slaughter and to the
cross and to sadism and algolagnia, to looting and
rubble. No one can elude the birth-sentence, which
tears you from the uterus and at the same time glues
you to the nipple. And who, once housed in that
nest and nourished by that free fruit, can adapt
himself to the common territory, where you have to
fight for any food and any shelter? Accustomed to
an enchanting fusion, believing it eternal, and
certain of a joyous gratitude for his own ingenuous
offer, the beginner will blanch, amazed, at his
encounter with alienness and terrestrial indifference; and then he will turn into brute or servant.
Even stray animals seek, more than food, caresses,
spoiled, even they, by the mother who licked them
as cubs day and night, above and below. For her

teat and her tongue, no merits were required. Nor was adornment needed to appeal to her.

"You will go in shame of your nakedness." And here the first big autocrat neglected to add "and you will need caresses until your last day," whereas in reality, with this unspoken law, he was reaffirming his own established injustice. Favored, in fact, among mortals are the beautiful and the young, who can offer without shame their own radiant flesh to caress. And also redeemed are those who can offer, at least, some other display to make themselves attractive: champions, for example, thaumaturges, poets. But I? I have nothing to offer. No decoration to unfurl over my shame, not even a championship of the lowest league, no cheap miracle, no song on the radio. I am a bourgeois puppet, disarmed and wrecked, a shadow target for a shooting gallery. We can laugh about it together, Aracoeli!

But you, Mamita, help me. As mother cats do with their ill-born kittens, eat me again. Receive my deformity in your pitying abyss.

Translated by William Weaver

THE BENEDICTINES
by
Maria Occhipinti

The crossing from Ustica to Palermo took four hours, and there was a magnificent sunset over the sea. My baby was in perfect health at the time, growing bigger every day. Upon landing we were taken to our destination by horse-carriage. S. and my fellow villager got off at the Ucciardone prison near the port, whereas I was taken to the Benedictines, the women's prison of Palermo. As soon as I was inside, the head-guard took my fingerprints. A few of the Benedictine nuns and an elderly female guard drew near, curiously examining me and the child, both quite sun-tanned. We were searched and assigned to the maternity ward.

This was a large dormitory with cement-blocked windows, the type you can find in any other prison, and there was a stifling stench as in a hencoop. The washing was hung indoors where the sun never reached. While awaiting our turn at the wash tub, we would stand there hugging our dirty pile of baby togs. There were no cradles. The mothers and the children slept together on miserable urine-soaked pallets made of lumpy, smelly horsehair. When there weren't enough beds, the women had to sleep on the floor on old threadbare blankets. When pillows were too few to go around, even for the babies, the hard mattress was folded slightly to support the child's tender head. Whenever a woman with a pillow was due to leave, the others tried to reserve it long beforehand. But only one could be lucky. My baby and I spent more than five months without a pillow. Sleeping was also difficult because most of the children cried at night, one after the other, as if taking turns.

The food cooked by the nuns was disgusting. They often served us hard unchewable peas, which we, just for the fun of it, made into bracelets, necklaces and even rosaries. We often found ants in the soup and there were never more than twenty bits of short pasta in those watery slops. On Sundays, when they didn't serve meat, they would give us a taste of canned salmon or an egg, usually rotten. Evaporated milk was handed out in the morning, and we got a quarter of a glass more than the other prisoners. We were also given an extra ladleful of broth at lunch and an extra hundred grams of bread apiece. But if you didn't get bread in from the outside, you were bound to go hungry. For the babies' hygiene there was a cubicle adjoining the dormitory, the so-called delivery room, with wash-tubs and gas heating, but only on the occasion of a delivery would the nun deem it necessary to bathe the newborn babe a few times. Her only concern was to baptize it. A former prisoner had left behind, as a memento, a lovely hand-embroidered baby dress, and each newborn child wore that at the christening.

Besides the two women-guards, the staff consisted of two wardens and a head warden. Then there were the nuns: one was the door-keeper, another, by the name of Santa Lucia, accompanied

us when we went "to take air." The Institute
belonged to the French nuns of the Sacred Heart
Order and they were all to be addressed as Saint or
My Mother. Saint Ignazia was assigned to the
maternity ward and to the pharmacy. Matters of
daily discipline, such as the distribution of meals,
punishments, etc., were the domain of My Mother
Antonietta who was short and dark with bright
black eyes and who never hesitated to send us into
solitary confinement for a trifle. She was called
the Marshal and had been at her post for twenty
years.

Each morning a guard came in with a bucket of
warm water, dispensing two ladlefuls apiece to
wash our babies with. We never took a bath. Once
I complained about this to the Mother Superior
who granted us audiences on Thursdays. The
Reverend Mother had a soft gentle voice, tremulous
and endearing, but deep inside she was just the
opposite. Heavy-set, old and decrepit, she was
always escorted by two nuns. She would welcome
us with feigned tenderness, make us promises
galore, but we never obtained a single thing from
her.

In a sort of store-room upstairs, there was a
faucet with a basin underneath as large as a holy
water font in church. In order to wash, we had to
kneel down on the rough cement floor. I explained
to the Mother Superior that we couldn't go on like
that because of the many diseases that circulate in a
prison, syphilis among others. It wasn't sanitary
nor was it humane to make us wash our children's
clothing where the prostitutes scrubbed their
underwear. I requested a separate tub for the
maternity ward. Although there was a large laundry

room on the ground floor, we were not allowed to enter it. The nuns and the guards used it for their own convenience. Those prisoners who had to serve long sentences preferred to labor there as laundresses rather than remain locked up inside their cells.

They would give us no semolina or soft bread to prepare our babies' night-feedings – only stale bread that was brought in on an open cart, exposed to dust and flies. This was counted out at the door and then thrown down on the floor, in a corner. Later, a custodian distributed it to us out of her large apron. The nuns knew very well where the bread was put and yet they never took the trouble to get a basket.

Since the warden's permission was needed in order to have a little pastina for the children, we began to shift for ourselves. By placing two tin cups on the floor of the lavatory (we, in the maternity ward, had a lavatory) together with some of the horsehair from a mattress (the least dilapidated, so that it wouldn't smoke too much) we would start a fire and manage to cook the baby food. The stall gradually smelled of smoke and the head warden, noticing it, came and asked why and scolded us for it.

I spoke up: "Isn't it enough for you to treat our children worse than animals? Must you even scold us on top of it?"

Naturally I was put in solitary confinement; the Marshal taking me there "all in the name of God."

There were three cells situated to the right of the chapel. A partition of wood that reached almost to the ceiling acted as a dividing wall. In the hallway, packed in between the partition and the cells, were piles of dirty bed linen mixed up with extra mattresses and worn-out blankets. In the farthest cell a nun had died in a bomb attack, and it was said you could see ghosts in there. So some of the inmates were afraid to spend the night in that cell. Once a fifteen-year old girl who had been locked in there started to wail and cry hysterically as nighttime came. The nun's bedroom was right across the hall on the left side of the chapel, but she heard nothing. Only when we started to curse and beat our clogs against the iron gate did she finally arrive, barely awake, but she refused to let the girl out. So it was not until a fellow prisoner and I were allowed to go into the cell to keep her company that the girl calmed down and fell asleep. There was no mattress or sheets to be had in solitary confinement, only a plank for a bed and a wooden board for a pillow.

My punishments always lasted three or four days. My child would be kept in the dormitory and brought in only at breast-feeding time. At night, however, she would sleep with me, and so as not to make her suffer, I would hold her over my stomach and prop her up among the blankets, remaining almost uncovered myself. The nun would come on a nightly inspection carrying a flashlight. Near the top of the door was a window wide enough to sit in. Thus, during the day, I would clamber up the steel door, sit there and read, holding onto the bars in order not to fall.

You had to get permission from the Mother Superior in order to leave the cell. The head warden was not vindictive, after all he was a father and a Neapolitan. Of the wardens, the older was wicked and rude, the younger one, as good as gold;

but even the nasty one was more humane than the nuns. You weren't allowed out of the cell without first begging the Mother Superior's forgiveness and kissing her hand. Since I was firmly convinced that I had done no wrong, I could not stoop to hand-kissing. I would not be a hypocrite and so I had to remain five days longer in the cell. The warden himself came to try to convince me, but realizing I would not yield, he let me out that same night. My reasoning was: "Shouldn't they be the ones to have some understanding for us?" Sometimes we swore against God because of our great suffering, and we would be severely punished, "all in defense of God." But I never thought God needed *them* to defend himself. We were punished enough by God by simply being in that place. Why aggravate our punishment? By increasing our pain, the nuns only made us poor women more bitter, and instead of saving us they just speeded up their own damnation.

I recall that one morning I had left my child in bed while I went to wash the mess tin. On my return, I found the child covered with excrement up to her face. Not knowing how to cope, I quickly called the guard who came with a nun; the nuns always pretended not to hear our calls. Only when some of the inmates, out of anger, started shouting: "BITCHES! BITCHES!" would they run in. That insult was enough to make them come. So in they marched, telling me there was no hot water in the kitchen and that I would have to wait for the second shift, at 4 pm. In despair, I snatched a sheet from the bed, put the two tin cups in the middle of the room with the bucket over them, tore up the sheet in a hundred shreds, and set a match to it, warming the water with that fire. The nun and the guard watched the scene. That night, although in solitary confinement, I was satisfied, even though the matter of forgiveness had to be gone through all over again.

Seeing that I wore a Communist badge and kept pictures of Stalin and Lenin near my bed, they gave political significance to my every gesture, and so insisted that I bow to them; but it was entirely my conscience that dictated my actions, not political or party principles. That time my punishment lasted eight days, but I remained calm. My inmate-friends brought me food, and I didn't suffer too much. Whenever I found a piece of coal I would write on the wall: DOWN WITH THE HYPOCRISY OF THE NUNS! JUSTICE WILL TRIUMPH! and other such phrases. When the warden passed through on inspection, at the sight of the graffiti, he would pull out a flashlight from his pocket to read them better, but he never said anything. On one wall I wrote that nuns were unworthy of carrying Christ over their breast. With time enough to meditate, I never grew desperate.

One Sunday morning during Mass I was perched up in my usual spot in the cell from where I could see everything. When the priest started preaching about how Christianity was the religion of pity and charity, I listened patiently for a while, but all of a sudden my emotions got the best of me and I found myself shouting: "There's no charity here, there's no goodness. Here a mother is punished for rebelling against having her child suffer." A sort of panic stirred in the chapel. My inmate-pals were overjoyed and some begged the priest: "Forgive her, let her out, she's a mother." I was out of the cell in the evening.

That week the head director of the Ucciardone prison, who was also our director, came on a visit. The nuns received him with the usual smiles and bows. All dressed in white, they were like doves fluttering about the man. The director received us in his office, but the Mother Superior was always present at these meetings, so we could never really express ourselves freely. There was always a Guardian Angel following and watching us everywhere. Nonetheless, I decided to try something, so I asked to be received by the director. In the room were Mother Marshal and Mother Superior. As soon as the latter understood my intention when I broached the subject concerning the reforms necessary, she interrupted me, smiling: "Pardon me, director, there are a few things I might say about Occhipinti – but I'll let them pass...."

This was meant to prevent me from continuing, to keep me from voicing the rest of the truths I had started to acquaint the director with. I wondered: "Why is she hindering me like this? Why will she punish me when the director has left?" Not letting her daunt me, I continued, confessing to having torn up the sheet in shreds to clean my child. I said that, for my child's sake, I was ready to undergo any type of punishment, but that I hadn't committed any wrongdoing whatsoever. I told him about the baby-feedings, showed him the mess tin and how seventy grams of pasta did not amount to more than twenty tiny pasta rings, showed him the vegetables, hard cauliflower stalks only good for rabbits, peas that could serve as necklace beads, and told him that was how it was every day. Even the girls from Palermo could receive food from the outside on

Thursdays and Sundays only. How long could it be possible to hold out without becoming ill? In what kind of a state would we be when we left the place? But why didn't the Mother Superior intercede for me instead of flashing her eyes at me so ferociously? The director would not believe me about the quantity of pasta. The Marshal said I had eaten it, but was later proven wrong by the other protesting prisoners. The director saw the ants, too. The nuns said they were insects that were in the olive oil, but then couldn't they have run it through a sieve with gauze cloth, and treated us more humanely? Why was the management of the institution completely entrusted to them? Wouldn't we, the mothers, have done better? At the Ucciardone prison the inmates themselves controlled the house organization. I asked for inmate control at the Benedictines', too – for one of us to be present in the kitchen, but it wasn't granted. Just for a couple of days a guard was sent from the Ucciardone prison. He would accompany the nun who distributed the soup. With the ladle they would fish out of the kettle the same quantity of pasta as on all the previous days.

"Don't you see?" the Marshal exclaimed, "with the guard present we weighed the pasta and put it all in the pot. And it's the very same quantity as yesterday. Are you convinced now that we always cook the same quantity of pasta?"

"Liar, you're a hypocrite too," I shouted to the guard. "These are not seventy grams of pasta per person!"

The fact of the matter was that our ration of food had to suffice for the feeding of the orphans, too, and this was the explanation of the mystery. I insisted on having one of us to check in the kitchen. The women wanted it to be me, but this was totally unrealistic. The nuns' excuse was that we might escape from the kitchen.

Behind our dormitory was the delivery room with two basins for the newborn babies, running water, and a bed with a hard mattress for women in labor to lie on. The midwife was called at the onset of labor pains, one of us acting as the assistant. The midwife, Miss R., knew her job well. By telling spicy jokes she managed to encourage the woman in labor while keeping the others merry. One night around ten o'clock, from my gate I heard someone moaning. It was an inmate in labor. The guard let her lie on the bed while a warden went to call the midwife. A new being was about to be born, but there was no hot water. The kitchen was locked and the guard could not open it, nor could she waken the nuns. As usual, we managed to adapt to the circumstances. We were not to produce any smoke and there was little paper. In order to waste no time, I held the basin close over the flames with my hands, while another woman placed the pieces of paper underneath. Towards the end, I could feel my fingers burning. At times like that we all helped each other with love. We washed both mother and child, but she caught an infection and it was a miracle that she survived. The sanitary napkins for the mother were just poorly rinsed dirty rags. No special diet. Rarely were they kind enough to cook any baby food, but even then it would be brought in either cold, burnt or salty.

We all had our own ways of escaping from all that sadness. We might sing, sew by day and night, contrive to handcraft slippers for the little ones: by using remnants of old blankets for the soles, shortening the sheets to serve as the uppers, removing the thread from the sheets in order to embellish the slippers with quaint embroidery. We even had a razor blade, a pair of scissors, files and knives made from tins, but heaven help us should we get caught. As soon as a suspicious sound was heard (a nun or a guard drawing near) a magic word ran through the dormitory: "Muff, muff," and everything disappeared inside our bosoms.

As in all the other churches, a priest came to our chapel to preach during the Lenten season. The Mother Superior never missed a sermon, always keeping her eyes fixed on the wan faces of the women prisoners. She observed us every day, she could witness the state we were in, but the way we were treated never changed. She probably thought we should feel fortunate if, in spite of all our sins, we succeeded in staying alive. Perhaps to her eyes we all looked in pretty good health.

After the sermon, they made us sing a little song telling of Christ's passion. It sounded like a lament springing from so many bleeding hearts. Each stanza ended with the refrain:

> Because of my sins, O Jesus,
> Forgive me, have mercy on me.

At the end, the priest would make each one of us kiss the Crucifix, after which, in single file, the guard would send us back to our dormitories. To me all that cross-kissing was unacceptable. I hated being obliged to do it, all that pretentious humbug, but most of all the lack of hygiene, for all of our two hundred mouths touched the same spot, and the place swarmed with syphilis.

Whenever the nuns called me an atheist or a non-believer, I always answered that I was far more religious than they. They knew very well that each evening I shared with a friend the piece of bread I earned by preparing the altar cloths or sewing the Mother Superior's linen or the dresses for the orphans. Having chosen to suffer when I was a young girl, I had stood before the altar in the Ecce Homo Church and implored God for his thorns, his cross, his martyrdom. This was why I always went to extremes in everything, because I had modeled myself after Christ, and Communism, for me, was none other than a way of sacrificing myself for the love of others.

At Easter time, I, too, went to Confession, but it was more like a conversation with the priest. I told him he had better convert the nuns, because we were already suffering enough. We had too much suffering to be able to hate. At the Mother Superior's celebration party, for example, we were the first to extend our hands to those who tormented us. On that occasion, the whole prison became involved. The dormitory cells were decorated to look like parlors. We vied with each other in preparing the prettiest embroidery. The day before there was a general cleanup. On the feast day, we spread all the blankets on the floor as a carpet for the Superior to walk over. Out of a little fur jacket I improvised a soft cushion. I even wrote a poem to read at her arrival and we all waited anxiously.

Then a nun burst in saying: "Quick, quick, Mother is coming!"

But the Mother didn't appear. An hour went by, then two; the whole morning passed by. We waited for her all afternoon. At a certain point we were told that the prefect of the city had come and taken her to his house in a limousine. Full of resentment, I asked for paper, pen and inkstand, and wrote a letter my way, telling her she had humiliated us by treating us as habitual criminals, whereas our wishes had been most sincere, and that Christ himself had recognized that the last shall be first. The Mother Superior sent her apologies by a nun, letting us know that she hadn't done it on purpose.

As the remains of certain ruins retain a part of their former splendor that is worthy of contemplation and admiration, those "immoral" creatures, the prisoners, also have souls that are worth study and meditation, for all has not been lost. Public condemnation is not so overwhelming for them. Although unconsciously, they somehow realize what a precious heritage they possess and this accounts for their survival, even though they are despised by society at large. The prostitute, thief, and killer, so feared and detested, are at heart just as weak and frightened as all other women.

Almost always illiterate, chronic offenders will trust their parents alone. This typically regional attitude may be traced to the three main tenets of the Sicilian upbringing: first of all, hatred of the police; secondly, vendetta in the case of betrayed love; and, thirdly, obedience to family authority. The family, however, is in no position to impart education, and the government intervenes only to increase the police force. What people need, however, is employment, together with schools, housing and hospitals – not more police. Once people are given the possibility of learning about other civilizations, of gaining a new concept of life, they will understand that vindication is barbaric and useless. They need to be helped to see what is still savage inside their hearts and have their latent sensitivity awakened in order to see the horror of their actions. They do indeed have consciences and do not feel at all so powerful as one might think. All the male delinquents I have met are weak creatures, more afraid than others, perhaps. This is why the criminal adores his mother and clings to her desperately. Knowing what a dangerous life he leads and conscious of the fact that his girlfriend or wife may turn him in or tire of the relationship, he is well aware that he will be alone as he trudges through life, and so he feels the need for attachment to his mother. To him Mother means more than God. Many were the fellows I saw at prison visiting-time who burst into tears as soon as they saw "Mama" enter. In the silence of their cells, they would call out for her with their whole soul, for that is where the criminal loses all his inhibitions and self-esteem, and he will cry like a baby. He is no longer the brute who horrified the newspaper readers. He needed a weapon in order to feel strong; and it was the weapon that made him strong.

The Sicilian does not combat the State or his boss by using his intelligence, for that is not part of his cultural formation; his only means of expression is a knife or a gun, with which he gives vent merely to weakness and ignorance. Just as Christ said: these poor wretches know not what they do. And when they implore God before a crime so that everything will work out well, that simply proves how unsure and afraid they are.

After a year and a half of detention we were all anxiously awaiting the national referendum on June 2nd because a Republic would mean amnesty for us political prisoners. After the Republic had been voted in, the Minister of Justice, who was then Togliatti, sent a telegram in late June with orders to release us. It was a damp, hot afternoon when I was summoned to the head office. The warden read the telegram, but then added maliciously, that I was to remain in prison to expiate another crime. What a terrible blow! I rebelled, asking what the other crime was, thinking it was probably on account of that sheet I had torn to shreds and set on fire. I even wrote a petition to the Judge of Appeals that I wished to be told why I was being kept in prison. Several months passed by with neither answer nor interrogation. My family expected me from day to day, not knowing whether I was being kept pending a trial for what happened on that January 6th before I was arrested, or for other reasons. I wrote home saying that I had no idea why I, together with five others, was being kept. Only after my father engaged a young lawyer did we discover that I had been implicated in a crime of extortion: two inmates had fought over two hundred lire! But I had taken no part in the argument and was able to prove it when the investigating judge came and questioned me. Two days later I was set free.

I had no husband to go home to, since he, expecting I would serve a long sentence, had gone to live with another woman. With that particular cycle in my life ended, I was truly free, liberated from all the burden of prejudice. But I felt like a fragile empty shell in the middle of an immense ocean. Obliged to face the problems of daily survival and of giving my daughter different cultural values, I wandered through various cities of Italy, enriching my store of experiences, meeting new people with other ways of thinking and customs. I even went to Switzerland and after I saw, first-hand, what an adult civilization was like, and witnessed a more modern conception of love, liberty and self-respect, the men of my homeland appeared to me extremely immature; barely at the crawling stage.

What remains in my heart, after so much disappointment and bitterness, is the sweet indelible memory of the Sicilian women who did not rebel as I did, who know how to serve their husband-owners with common sense, and can even feel compassion toward their men – all the while, waiting hopefully for things to change for them, too.

Translated by Gloria Italiano

THE TREE
by
Anna Maria Ortese

Last Saturday, as the first snow began to fall, which was just towards five in the afternoon, I found myself at the Central Station, having accompanied a person to a train. At first, I didn't even realize it was snowing, but it struck me, once again in the open, that something in the tone and color of the great, broad square before the station had slightly changed. It was the very same square that all of us can see at any hour of the day or night, to the right the large hotel surmounted by a flattened dome, and the tramway tracks on the left, leading towards the center of town past a variety of cafés where brightly lit windows open back through a whitish haze to a glimpse of the reds and yellows of bottles of liqueurs. But the cafés, and I grasped it only after a moment or so, were all dark and empty, though open, and no trams were running, not so much as the most distant clanging of their bells. I thought there must have been a power failure in this part of the city, perhaps elsewhere as well, and I made up my mind to go back to my hotel on foot. After all, it was not very far away, and the weather wasn't cold.

As I looked about, a little bewildered, in search of the street to take (at least ten streets run out from this square) that indistinct sensation of just a few moments before came back to me, but now with the weight of a real disturbance: the sensation that something abnormal had taken place. Where I found myself was not Milan, no more than Hamlet and Ophelia are citizens of England. The plain looking houses that rise up in the many streets around the square had an evanescence, and a heart-rending pallor. Their walls seemed to shine from some interior source and were no longer lit by starlight, nor by any ray of brightness belonging to the world of our own. "It must always be like this, at certain hours of the year, and for me to realize it now is to be explained by a particular fragility of my nerves."

I started down Via P., from which I would then cross Piazza Grande and reach my hotel. And I once again, skirting close to the walls, felt strangely intent, like a person who had just received an important piece of news, something concerning one's own personal life, only shortly before. But, to tell the truth, I couldn't remember what that news might have been; so my calm began little by little to creak and give way like a sheet of ice over a stream of warm, black water murmuring and fleeing beneath it.

"Let's see," I said to myself. "The hotel. Everything there okay. The bill paid up. Work to do for tomorrow...quite fine. Let's see what else." And then, suddenly, I grasped the reason for that sense of dismay I had felt at the exit from the station. My dismay lay in a fact that was quite entirely banal, yet alarming: I no longer had any idea of whom I had accompanied to the station.

"But nothing could be more normal," I remarked to myself after a moment of reflection. "When we're especially fatigued, even the name of what month it is, or of the season, can slip our minds. Maybe it wasn't even an important name. At any rate, I'll recall it again in a moment."

I wanted to give myself a rational explanation for what had occurred, but as soon as I had put my finger on it, I ceased to be at peace, and I might have said that a mouse had slipped inside my dress and found its way up close to my heart, where at first it nibbled tenderly and then with greater zeal, striking deeper. Finally it bit to the pulse and the seat of life itself, and I felt a lacerating pain.

The mouse fled. I saw it run away directly from in front of me and then across the street to hide at the curb, from where it watched me with a strange, flashing brightness in the tiny pupils of its eyes. But even though the pain was still horrid and the beast right there, I refused to own up to it. "The weather is really changing," I remarked to myself. "This twinge is a warning. I'll drink a small cup of hot rum as soon as I'm back in my room."

I began to feel cold, but paid it no attention as I trained my eyes upwards here and there onto those buildings that looked so dead while yet suffused with a vague spark of dawn, an uncertain reflection, those facades where not a single door or window stood unshuttered to allow the glimpse of a face, a light, and where not a single voice resounded, not a sound, not even the lightest sound, of passing footsteps. "At this hour, in Milan, everyone is asleep," I continued to spin out to myself. "It's a city of workers. They go to bed early, by nine o'clock."

At that point, a clock from a distant church, a clock, seemingly, that wasn't quite sure of this world and the clapper of which resounded with a clear, grave music, struck five hours and two quarters.

"There's one of those clocks that gets stuck," I mumbled after a moment.

I reached the park, and here I realized that it was really snowing, quite heavily. The snow fell from the sky like a whirlpool of light, and when looked at steadily, it gave the impression of swirling back upwards. It rose and fell. How beautiful it was! It didn't touch the ground, and its large, transparent flakes just barely caressed the branches of certain trees and then melted away. It seemed a hand that wants to write out something immense and portentous, or to stroke a forehead, and that continually repents, trembles, and vanishes. One felt a vague, profound desire to be ravished into that raiment of light, to hover upwards from the black earth and flee into a place made only of serenity, music, and joy. And why was that not to happen?

There was a bench, and I approached it. I sat down, and remained there quietly to look around me as I held the upturned collar of my coat tight against my face. In the spinnings and reversals of that eddying of white, inside that magnificent calm, as though a mantle of white velvet were rushing to fold itself around the world, I reheard a remote and harmonious echo of that clock, a song of hours. Any number of memories unwound through my mind, but without fever. I saw my mother and my father, early mornings in the sunlit garden, I listened to the ceaseless sound of the March wind on the hill. Then, at a certain point, all these images and sounds of light disappeared, and I saw myself again in this city, in my hotel room as I prepared to go out and turned off all the lights....Yes, *all the lights suddenly went out,* and my mind lapsed back into its great confusion, and again that sensation of a brutal pain at my heart. Something must surely have happened, there was no longer room for doubt.

I would have given anything at all to have been left unreminded of it, and to let everything remain exactly as it was, with neither form nor name. I got up from the bench, and, vacillating, fixing my eyes as best I could in front of me, I set out to where I thought I would find the exit.

But the exit was no longer there, or at least it couldn't be seen because of the snow that had fallen. However, there was a great number of trees: their black, twisted roots came almost up from out of the ground, and some of them seemed to be human beings – human beings deprived of everything and at the end of their lives, and who huddled now against a wall and cried. In pure and absolute silence, the snow continued to fall on these creatures. I walked in the midst of them, and would have said that they silently stepped aside to allow me through. Never before, here in the park, had I realized that there were so many trees, and all so sensitive. The sight of them began to feel oppressive, and to frighten me. Why were they suffering? I felt quite fine, entirely fine. No, it wasn't because of me.

"The hotel should be somewhere close by," I began again to repeat to myself with absurd intensity. "The windows will all of course be dark, but the entrance will be bright and full of people.

There's Corrado, Daniele, the lovely Iris, the others."

A sign, quite large and just like the ones that parade one after the other along the highways, hung at the top of a pole fixed into the earth, and gigantic letters, in a sharp, bright green, spelled out these words before my eyes:

"SILENCE. DISAPPEARED. TRANQUILITY."

"Disappeared" was the word I stared at most, entranced, much more than at the others. It awakened my heart to such a depth of echoes and suspicions as to arouse a true terror that sucked all the heat from my forehead, and for an instant I was embraced with immobility itself.

"So even now," I continued, while breathing a sigh that released me from this horror, "they insist on putting up signs on the grass, as though that hadn't been proved already to be so entirely useless...." As I said this, my eyes, which were full of tears for which there was absolutely no reason, ranged off into the distance to a large open space where, once, a small monument to Cavour had stood. The small monument was no longer there, and in its place was a dazzling tree, rising up to a great height.

This time I said nothing; but as I shook myself together, pushing away the anxiety that like a crazed bird dashed against the walls of my skull, I looked at this solitary, towering tree of ice that stood before me and I attempted to see it as no more than an artificious and puerile Christmas tree. But those branches were decorated with nothing but ice, even the trunk was covered with ice, and the peak burned with no light that wasn't a light of ice. Here and there from out of the whiteness hung sharp, pointed daggers of that muted blue that ice can take on, and they gleamed.

A supreme need to ignore the meaning of what was happening drew me to the base of that tree, gazing upwards, just like any other citizen, to admire its wintry transformation; and that was where I stood, smiling though both cold and full of pain, when the tree first moved: laden and sparkling with its burden of frost, it bent down and touched my forehead. I retreated, and the creature moved again.

Its roots had drawn out of the earth, like paws, and they weakly advanced within the light of the snow. They advanced to follow me. This, naturally enough, was a dream, though a horrid dream. So while hurrying my steps as best I could towards where I imagined the gates of the park to be, I set to repeating my eternal, monotonous, refrains: "Work, okay; tomorrow, Sunday...; phone Corrado...; let's see what else." As I ran these statements through my weakened, submerging mind, the apparition of ice and branches slithered up beside me on its pitiful roots and emitted a sound that I'm sure you could hardly have listened to without crying. It was just that various, profound, and finally similar to the story of a human life.

"These branches really do creak," I remarked from out of my obstinate compulsion to lie to myself, "but I would never have imagined that snow could be so much like metal. And, yes, it's of course that this tree has grown so light that the wind can carry it along like a leaf while making its boughs resound with such an enchanted noise...."

I began to run, while thinking these phrases, towards the gates, which stood there, I could see them, facing onto Via Boschetti. I came out into the street and then halted, though still with the sense that this supernatural creature of ice was just behind my shoulder, because my heart was about to explode. I was to see, however, that the tree was no longer there.

At that point, finally safe, I felt a faint desire to see and hear it once again, as though that conjunction of light and pain had held the hidden secret, the name, the thing, everything the nature of which I could not understand, that had made my heart that night go mad.

But I didn't see the tree again. Instead, here I was at Porta Venezia, and then Viale Vittorio Veneto, and the high embankment at the edge of the park, and my hotel.

This large, modern building, eighteen storeys tall, its walls wounded by over a thousand windows, stood before me, and I stopped. I exclaimed, "At last!" but with a voice that was broken by regret and by a longing for a truth from which I had subtracted myself, fearing to look it in the face; and simultaneously I was struck by something extraordinary.

To the front of the hotel atrium, where a little elevator ordinarily runs and where friends are always coming and going, to the front of this atrium now brightly lit but totally empty, two goldfinches of precisely the size of a human form were roosted on a branch covered with snow, a branch that issued from the wall above the glass door, almost as though the wall itself were earth and the hotel a forgotten garden.

Their small, round eyes, round and black, were fixed, bright, and melancholic; and a song both acute and I couldn't say if more sweet or full of desperation, a song that spoke of tenderness and farewell, of the hope of regaining the woods, and the doubt, and of a joy besieged by cold and nothingness, issued from their unmoving beaks. These birds were dead. With their fiery foreheads and black and yellow wings, and perched on delicate legs of a material that seemed to be gold, they were dead and already cold beneath their silken plumage. Their song, a memory. Faced with their gracefulness and their death, I then suddenly understood why the city was dark, why the mouse had gnawed at my heart, why the tree laden with ice had pulled itself up from the ground to come and offer me company, singing songs about the past. I understood *who* I had accompanied to the station, and *who* these two marvelous shadows of birds had to be. I understood as well that my youth, which I had attempted to forget with all my phrases saying "fine...let's see...the bills...fine...tomorrow...," I understood that my youth, and everything else that you too will have lost, had everywhere, that night, returned; frightened and full of sobs, it had run like a girl along this pitiful earth.

Translated by Henry Martin

PERFETTA'S DAY
by
Fabrizia Ramondino

Nonna will never go to heaven. Even if she dies, she won't be able to leave this room, this house, and this world.

She's here, sitting at the dining room table drinking coffee. For a week now she's given up dunking her biscuit in hot milk as she's always done. So much the better. This way she doesn't think of me and say: "Eat! Eat!" Who knows why milk and biscuits make her feel like bothering about me. Now she's drinking her coffee and, instead of looking at me, she's staring into space. If she were to stare more into space perhaps she could go to heaven. At least a good part of her could go. Nonna is so big.

Never did a wild rabbit come out from under her skirt the way it did with Signora Cianfrusaglia in the book *Masquerade,* which was given to us because the TV talked about it and which I'm looking at now. Never anything that could escape and go far away. Nothing of Nonna's has ever escaped from this house. And nothing can ever escape from this house, because nothing escapes Nonna.

I've finished the book and would like to stare into space, but I can't. If I do, Nonna, in a sing-song and fretful voice, says: "What are you doing? Why aren't you playing?" Besides, I can't even leave the room, Nonna doesn't want me to, she's afraid something will happen to me. Nothing must happen to me.

Here I am sitting on the floor on a scatter rug so she can't see much of me. The dining room table has legs which are bulgy at the top and then straight and thin, like Nonna's legs. It's made of a strange wood, sick-looking, with light and dark spots which are supposed to imitate marble. It reminds me of ice cream shaped like fried eggs and like spaghetti with tomato sauce, creations of a famous confectioner to whose shop I was once taken. Just looking at them repulsed me. The sideboard, the china closet, and the buffet are of the same wood; only two of the chairs are alike; over fifty years the other four got broken. Nonna always marvels that everything wasn't broken.

On the floor there's always a mess of things. Giulia says: "There are so many of us! I can never keep things clean and tidy!" We all came from Nonna. I call her Nonna but she's not my grandmother but my great-grandmother. Only Giulia the maid didn't come from Nonna. She's pale and thin, maybe she came from Nonna's shadow. Zio Augusto's wife didn't come from her either, but as she's always stuck to Zio Augusto, it seems as if she came from him, like Eve from Adam's rib, when they still weren't quite two people.

Gradually as the house fills up with people (I think we are fourteen now) the disorder grows, so Giulia says. "Now I'm at the end of my tether," she goes on. Or else she says, "But perhaps it's better this way. At this point it's definitely futile to begin putting things in order." Then she says, "Look how fate works...I've been in this house for forty years and what was once an upper-class home with bedrooms, study, entrance hall, salon, dining room now seems a *basso*.... I clean and clean and it just gets dirtier. Just like the rest of the world. Too many people...you can't imagine the lines in the shops and crowded streets at all hours...if you didn't know that people always come out from the same place, you'd ask where do they all come from?... I've stayed just the way Mamma made me. One I was and one I've stayed....

All over the floor, then, are all our toys, always all broken because they're in a jumble and everyone breaks everybody else's. Newspapers...Zio Eugenio reads the paper and leaves it on the floor. Sometimes he takes it into the toilet and then brings it back all wet. Once I went in after he came out; it stank of cigarettes and shit. He hadn't even pulled the chain and, since the toilet paper always runs out and often nobody put in a new roll for two days, the bowl was full of pieces of newspaper. Ever since then newspapers have that smell for me. Besides, that odor reaches here from the bathroom which is next to this room. Not only do they not flush, but they leave the door open, too.

On the floor are two cheese rinds. Massimo hides them behind the broken leg of the china closet for the mouse. He has a passion for mice, wants to start breeding white ones. But this mouse is no thoroughbred mouse. We can't figure out where he comes in. Once he climbed up on the window and my uncle tried to crush him with the shutter but didn't succeed.

Also on the floor are my cousins' schoolbooks. Before coming to this house, they lived in a foreign country and they learned to study stretched out on their stomachs. It seems that for them there's no difference between tables, chairs, beds. When they're studying, they get up to go make popcorn in the kitchen, leaving books and notebooks behind. "Come say your verbs with me," says Nonna.

The cousins come back with a bowl of popcorn, lean over to pick up a book and some popcorn spills out on the floor. They hand the book to Nonna who begins to query them on the verbs. Trying to peek at the page over Nonna's shoulders, they get distracted and tip the bowl, spilling the popcorn on the floor again. But there's never any popcorn on the floor because they pick it right up and eat it. Massimo picks it up with his thumb, squashing it a little.

Nonna knows all the verbs by heart. My cousins recite them sing-song, but Nonna always uses a solemn voice as if she were praying. It seems that if there weren't any verbs, the entire castle of words would crumble. When it comes to Latin verbs, Nonna's voice becomes even more solemn. Then she lifts her chin and gravely nods her head as she pronounces them. The true bones that hold up Nonna's great mass are verbs. It's as if she puts on a mask for their recitation and when she's got this mask on, it seems to me that finally she has definite contours, that she's not all gelatin. In that moment she is detached from all the things she was hideously stuck to. But this happens rarely. My cousins flee verbs like the enemy. They're big kids and they escape to the street.

Now Nonna has finished her coffee and calls, "Giulia! Giulia!" in a worn-out voice. As usual, Giulia answers, "I'm coming! I'm coming!" and she doesn't come. Giulia likes to stay in the kitchen, like a snail in its shell. This is the most dangerous moment for me. Waiting for Giulia, Nonna might look at me and if she notices that I'm doing nothing, she'll feel obliged to busy herself with me. That's why I'm pretending to be absorbed in my doll play, though I haven't played with dolls for a year. Not since I decided that I didn't ever want a daughter so that I couldn't become like Nonna. I don't want to become anything more than what I am.

So I pretend to put her little dress on, wash her, comb her hair. I am the youngest of this household and all these things that I am doing for my doll have been done for fourteen people, Giulia excluded, for whom no one ever did anything, according to her, not even those who are dead now. Nevertheless, they still live here in this house. Great-grandfather's hat and cane are, in fact, still hanging on the coatrack in the hall, and in the bathroom the corner of the mirror is broken where Grandfather hit it with his razor by mistake. It's not really broken, just cracked, and every once in a while a little piece of glass falls out. "That piece of glass must be removed," someone always says, but nobody does it.

In the next room, on the other side of the wall that I'm leaning against now, Totó lived for several years. They called him Totó and not Antonio because when he was six months old he was so funny, making such weird faces that he made everyone laugh.

Actually, he was mentally retarded and nobody noticed right off. He died before I was born. He was the son of Zio Augusto. One of the reasons why Zio Augusto and his wife don't leave this house is because it reminds them of Totó and they don't want to forget him. "It seems to me," says Zio Augusto's wife, "that if we were to forget him, something really terrible could happen to us."

No one can enter that room now because Zio Eugenio's mastiff, Moby Dick, is shut up in there. After his wife died, this uncle moved here with his six kids so that Nonna could help him raise them. Moby Dick lived in a garden and he's not used to being shut up inside – that's why he has to stay in that little room.

When Zio comes home from work at night, he opens the door and takes the dog for a walk. He is enormous; at first he howled, now he only drools and licks Zio when he's let out. He has a very soft stomach which almost drags on the ground. Teresa, my oldest cousin, used to open the door and take the dog out but then she would forget to shut him up again or maybe she forgot on purpose. One time Nonna almost fainted from fright. Unless a strong man helps her, she isn't able to move from her chair. Teresa and the others had gone out. Terrified, Giulia shut herself in the kitchen. The dog settled here by us, lying down next to Nonna, big and soft, just like her.

For three hours Nonna didn't move or breathe, her face growing whiter and whiter. I just continued doing what I always do here on the floor. I even tiptoed to the bathroom. Nonna gave me a commanding glance, but I didn't understand if she wanted me to remain in the bathroom or to return. Being irresistibly attracted to the dog and to Nonna, I didn't want to stay in the bathroom at all.

Nonna couldn't even prevent anything from happening to me. For a moment I thought about going out into the street with my cousins. Nobody could have stopped me, but the force that drew me to the room was like a strong magnet. I remember sitting in my corner thinking about escaping but, as if bewitched, I couldn't do it. The front door of frosted glass is embellished with my great-grandfather's initials in clear glass. It appeared so far away to me, as if it were at the end of the earth, as if the world weren't round but endless, long and narrow like the hallway, and beyond the door was the universal abyss one could fall into.

From that day on Zio has taken the keys to that room with him whenever he goes out. At first the dog would jump up against our wall for hours – perhaps he knew that we were here – or against the door. He doesn't do that anymore, we don't hear him the whole day. When Zio opens up for him in the evening, he doesn't move. It's Zio who makes him get up with fond words, though sometimes he has to pull him up.

Through the keyhole I can see his big, immobile buttocks. He's stretched out with his face toward the little window. Sometimes from here I think I can hear him sob.

There are more and more things that Zio has to lock up before going out. He's now put a padlock on his handkerchief and underwear drawer. All his sons and daughters were taking his handkerchiefs and his underdrawers. When he had to go out to the office he could never find any clean ones.

Since there's already my Nonna, my real grandmother, Zio's sister, is like an aunt to me. In fact, I call her Zia-Nonna. She takes care of all our dirty laundry when she gets home from the office. With a sweet and plaintive voice, she calls on one of the older nephews or nieces to help her. She smells very nice, even her voice has a scent of mint and whoever falls prey to that scented voice helps her empty the sack of dirty laundry and separate it into the whites and the coloreds.

She moans that today there's no telling what color clothes can be because who ever heard of red underwear and white slacks for kids (one of my cousins likes white jeans, he's nearly shaved his head and says that he wants to wear all white like an oriental monk) and navy blue and brown towels, which may or may not run. Perplexed, she stands for a while before the mountain of clothes and, finally dividing them up somehow, she does the first load.

Later, after her rest, "a little nap" she calls it, she's back in the kitchen doing another load of laundry with the help of another nephew. While she goes into the dining room to smoke a cigarette by Nonna, the nephew gets himself some bread spread with olive oil in the kitchen and disappears into the street. "Who's going to hang out the clothes? Who is going to hang out the clothes?" reverberates the voice of Zia-Nonna from room to room. She goes on complaining a long time. But the cousins are all out in the street and the wet clothes sit there in the pail.

I don't know what miracle happens sometimes. Sooner or later someone hangs out the clothes. Not always, though. Sometimes they stay in the pail till the next day. Then there's no room for hanging out the next day's loads, not in the bathroom on the drying rack nor on the kitchen balcony. With so many people, two loads of wash have to be done every day. Then there are two or three pails of clothes. Those of the day before have to be hung out first or they go sour. It's the same thing with the bread, we have to eat the old first and never the fresh. Bread, in fact, is the only thing in the house that isn't calculated, and too much always gets bought.

Giulia is here at last, standing next to Nonna, wiping her hands on her apron. She is so used to always doing something that she doesn't know what to do with idle hands and she keeps wiping her hands long after they're dry. Nonna writes out the shopping list, starting with bread. The bread calculations, however, depend on the rest of the list. Every morning Nonna starts by saying, "What do you think, Giulia, three or four kilos of bread?" And every morning Giulia invariably answers, "It depends, Signora."

If we eat pasta or gattó or rice, we won't need much bread. But if we have broccoli or sweet peppers, we'll need lots of bread because my cousins don't like vegetables much. To get them to eat them, the bread is split open and the vegetables stuffed inside. Sometimes we have milk for supper and this requires lots of bread, too. With so many people in the house, cookies are out of the question. Even if we have veal stew there has to be lots of bread, otherwise nobody's hunger would be satisfied.

Now that there are more than fourteen of us, Giulia never suggests broccoli. Nonna does, though, because the doctor has told her to have a light supper: broccoli and mozzarella. When Nonna mentions broccoli, Giulia says it's time to scrub the wall and floor tiles. In truth, they never get scrubbed though they need it. But Nonna sweetly insists we have broccoli. "Broccoli, Giulia, is good for you, it's good for you. Especially good for *you*, Giulia, for your kidney stones."

Giulia finally lets herself be convinced and smiles broadly. She's like a lover protecting herself. The truth is that she loves broccoli very much, loves to buy it, trim and wash it, eat it. She always says the only shopping she enjoys doing is at the vegetable stall. When she was a child, the only grocery shopping done was at the vegetable stall. Who ever went into the delicatessen? She did for the first time when she came to work for the Signora, my Nonna. All they ever ate at her house were broccoli and cabbage in the winter, fava beans and peas in the spring, tomatoes, sweet peppers and eggplant in the summer. And bread. Her mother used a lot of oil, as if it were, Giulia says, "the Extreme Unction of the queen." Thus Nonna grumbles to Giulia, "Giulia, be sure ·not to put too much oil." And Giulia always answers, "You are right, Signora. I forget that we've all become kings and queens and that we turn our noses up at abundance."

It takes them an hour to decide the shopping to be done. Nonna has everything bought day by day, otherwise it all goes. For example, if she buys half a kilo of parmesan cheese, the next day it's all gone. That's why she orders only two hundred grams at a time. Nonna writes the list on a notebook using a carbon paper and another sheet underneath, which is for Giulia. Everything is divided by store because Giulia doesn't know how to read. *SALUMIERE,* like the title of a fairy tale, is followed by a list of things to buy at the deli.

Giulia can read *SALUMIERE* because she's seen it written so many times along the street.

While Giulia is out shopping, there is no escape for me. Nonna wants me sitting right next to her and wants me to practice my penmanship by drawing little rods or a page of O's. I know how to write whole words but Nonna makes me practice every day with rods and O's until, she says, the rods are all straight and all the O's, all of them, are round, like the O in Giotto.

What will happen to me if I never in all my life learn to do them right? And what will happen to me if I do? Nonna says that the discipline of the spirit can be seen in one's handwriting and in the steadiness of one's hand. A musician, too, must have a steady and precise hand just like a watchmaker, says Nonna. She wants me to color without going outside the lines, too. I can't understand how Nonna, so shapeless that you don't know where she begins and where she ends, can think of making me do things of such precision.

Nonna has to have everything handy next to her because to get her upright and walking requires a very strong and calm person. Only Zio Eugenio can do it so she has to wait until he gets home in the evening. My big cousins tried once to lift her. "Come on, Nonna," they cried. Nonna got frightened because she was sure they were about to let her fall. Zio Augusto can manage it only in moments of great urgency. Nonna says he's becoming like a woman, always attached as he is to his wife.

After I'd been making O's, rods, a few words and even a few whole sentences for about an hour, Nonna turns around very slowly in her revolving chair and gropes around on the buffet behind her for

Mr. Tommaseo's Dictionary of the Italian Language.

I call him Mr. Tommaseo because for a long time I thought he was an old friend of my aunt who came to see her every so often. You see, they sometimes speak in Latin so we can't understand. It is very important to Nonna that she teach me words and all their meanings. This is the only part of the day, the only part of Nonna and of the world that I care about.

Nonna opens the dictionary at random. I wait for the surprise. Often it opens to the same pages, but Nonna's mind is like a steel trap, and, in irritation, she shuts the book immediately, ruffles the pages a little, blows on them and opens it again. Let's say the word "tongue" comes up. Nonna begins a rapid interrogation: "Where is your tongue? Show me it! What tongue do you speak? Do you like ox tongue or do you want to eat a tongue of land? What's the tongue of a shoe? Is your tongue coated? Does your tongue wag too much?"

She's like a witch gone crazy! Quickly back and forth in the dictionary she goes, pronouncing her abracadabra. For this reason, too, I say that Nonna is not alone in this room and in this house, because from her revolving chair she gives names to everything in the world. She can never die until all the shoe tongues disappear from fashion and the last tongue of land has sunk.

About an hour and a half or two hours later Giulia returns. Only when someone arrives can I leave the room and go to the entrance hall. Giulia smells like the outside, especially the vegetables she carries. She's so small and thin that she is lost

beneath the two huge shopping bags. Poking out of
one are the long loaves of bread and from the other,
parsley and other herbs. Today the vegetables and
fruit arc all wet. Perhaps it rained this morning and
I didn't notice. Since my cousins hung on the
drapes and broke the valance and the wooden rod,
Nonna keeps the shutters closed so that the
neighbors can't look in. In spite of the expense, we
have the electric lights on. Everyone here says that,
sooner or later, someone will fix the drapes.
Watching rain is the second best thing I like in the
world.

Giulia opens all the bags and packages on the
dining room table and Nonna checks it all: the
weight, the price, the quality. This is the only way,
Nonna says, to get by on the money we have. And
now, not even twenty-thousand lire a day are
enough. "When I was young and teaching school,"
says Nonna, "I wasn't able to do all this. Nearly
all my salary went for food. Often we didn't have a
hot meal and you spend much more if you don't do a
hot meal. Fortunately my mother came to live with
us and she checked everything as I do now. And
then we spent only two-thirds of my salary, even
though she meant an extra person."

Giulia consistently allows them to sell her
grated cheese which is rancid. She can't tell the
difference. She says she hasn't been able to smell
for several years. "Luckily," comments Nonna
weighing the mortadella on the scale, "there are a
lot of us and we have to buy in quantity, fifty grams
a person means nearly three-quarters of a kilo.
Percentage-wise, therefore, the weight of the paper
liner doesn't count much. Sometimes they use as
many as three liners: wax paper, heavy paper, and

167

then cellophane to make it look nice. When there were just four of us and we didn't buy large amounts, the weight of the paper counted for more than thirty percent.

I'd like to go into the kitchen to stay with Giulia but she shoos me out. She says she doesn't want anyone underfoot when she cooks, not even Zia-Nonna, should she want to help or keep Giulia company. Above all, she adds, I should keep in mind that in the forty years that she has been in this house never has any child been underfoot in the kitchen.

Forty years ago she made a pact with Nonna that she would see to everything. She would be housemaid, kitchen maid, and cook, but never a nursemaid. If one of the children enters her kitchen not only does she shoo him or her out, she goes to complain to Nonna immediately: "You know our pact. And you also know why I insisted on it. I raised four of my mother's kids and when the fifth was born, I had had it. I said, 'Mamma, I am going out to work as a maid and I'll give you my whole salary, but I'm done with raising children.' So if the child says it's fun to shell peas, I'll bring her here to *you* but she can't do it in the kitchen with me. You know I've never wanted anyone in the kitchen and you know why, too...." Standing in the door, she starts her speech all over again, sometimes three or four times over. Her face is beet-red because she's just left the stove or perhaps because she's indignant.

She goes on till Nonna gets irritated. If we've done the word "tongue" that day, Nonna shouts, "You evil tongue, you!" If we've done "tremble," it's "Tremble, Giulia!" If our word was "rigmarole," Nonna says, "Giulia, please, stop it with all this rigmarole." And if we haven't done an applicable word, she takes the wooden ruler (for which she has a thousand uses: to teach us to make straight lines, measure cloth, reach under the table for something, draw lines to make music paper for my cousin who is studying piano and solfeggio, scratch her legs which always itch because of bad circulation) and she raps it impatiently on the table. "Hear, hear!" Giulia says as she disappears into the kitchen. "Hear, hear!" Nonna repeats back and adds, "What a peasant!" or she starts laughing.

The dining room, where Nonna and I pass the day almost completely alone, at two in the afternoon fills up with practically the entire family: Zia-Nonna, who is really my grandmother; Zio Augusto, who fortunately comes home for lunch otherwise Nonna would have to wait for evening to go to the bathroom. She often says she doesn't want to drink anything so that she won't have to go to the bathroom. But sometimes she is unquenchably thirsty and then she can't wait.

Zio Augusto's wife is expecting another baby. Nonna keeps saying: "I had advised her against it: what if it comes out like Totó?" Then, getting mad, adds, "You know what she wants to name him, the fool? Guess! Guess! She wants to name him Totó. Now if that isn't inviting bad luck."

My mother is there, too. She goes back to work at three. Then my six older cousins. Zio Eugenio comes only at night and Zio Augusto has no control over my cousins who make a constant racket and have terrible table manners. "The mother's fault, poor thing. She was a foreigner and had other customs. In fact, no hot meals were cooked at their house," comments Nonna. "Perhaps only on Sunday. She used to make a dish she said was Dutch but it was identical to our veal stew with potatoes and carrots. Every other day the children ate sandwiches and milk and as many apples as they wanted, since she always had a basketful. They never sat at the table, everyone got what he wanted when he wanted it." It's unthinkable for most of my cousins to stay seated at the table to wait for the second course.

My great-grandfather, my grandfather and my father are not present because my great-grandfather is dead, my grandfather left his wife and children on the pretense of going to Rome to work and my father left my mother before I was born, nobody has ever explained why to me.

"Men," Nonna says, "are either boring like my husband was, once the honeymoon was over. Just as well I had my teaching. Or they're crazy like my daughter's husband or else think only of having a good time like your father." So I ask Nonna, "What about Zio Eugenio? And Zio Augusto?" "Augusto, don't you see it, is already so boring. And Eugenio is about to be driven crazy by his kids. How did he ever think of having six and these are modern times. Though I was born before this century began, I had only two! Who knows why they had so many. His wife wasn't low-born at all, she came from Amsterdam! Perhaps at that time people thought Paradise was about to come to earth, that over the world cornucopias would spill or that the tree of plenty was so tall and well-laden that they could all climb up it without coming to blows. See how your cousins fight over a piece of chocolate?

"And what can I say about the women, poor things? Fewer of them think only of having fun. Almost all of them are tedious, many are mental. But the tediousness of women is different from that of men, I think. It's much larger and deeper, it's ancient, ancient like that which comes to me from the crust of the earth. Luckily every so often they go mad. Look how tedious I am, always saying and doing the same things. Still the boredom I cause you is nothing next to that which I bring myself. And I've never had a moment of madness, never, in all my eighty-five years."

After lunch this is how Nonna begins talking with me. They all leave right away and the two of us are alone again. The signal is given by my cousins who push their chairs back noisily, leaving their napkins all bunched up and stained with sauce on the table or on the floor. My mother hugs me and has to leave right away. In exchange she brings me a present every night.

To accommodate so many people, the table has been pulled out and extra leaves added. I sit squeezed against the glass door of the china closet. I am stuck here. Until Giulia comes to clear the table, I cannot move. If I try to get down or to slide under the table, I might hit the glass with my elbow or strike it with my foot, break it and hurt myself. That's what my cousins would have done. That's why I was seated there, because I'm not like my cousins. I'm not boisterous and I never break anything.

Giulia takes a long time to get here. She's first got to put some order in the kitchen, on the table and on the drainboard. If she doesn't she won't know where to put the things she clears away from the dining room. Nonna sits opposite me at the other end of the table. We're far apart but she can't help but see me. So she chats on to me. The meal energizes her. After eating, she talks continuously until her head nods and she falls asleep.

"I will never go to heaven," she goes on. "Can you see me going up to heaven with my weight? I can't even get to the door to go out of the house. I'd need twenty angels and archangels, stronger than the men who carry the Lilies at Nola's feastday, to get me up to heaven. Even if I die, I won't be able to leave this house, let alone this world....

"All the people and all the things in the house are attached to me and carry my imprint. Their souls I have modelled like wax. You'll see that the day after my death, your grandmother Linda will sit right here, in my very place and will become just like me.

"And in the little next room there'll always be someone, a monster, like this awful mastiff Moby Dick who pants all day, unable to move at all, foaming saliva and looking out the window. My paralyzed mother was there first, then poor little Totó, now the dog. If Eugenio gets rid of him as he's promised, if he sells him to that friend of his who lives in the country or even lends him to him, you'll see, someone else will move in there.

"Your cousins have talked about putting a white mouse farm in there – 'our fondest dream,' they say. It would be loads of fun and also practical, according to them, because they could sell them to other kids and to a biological lab where they know a technician. They met him at judo and he said not this year as there is already someone who is supplying them, but next year they can go hunt cats in the alleyways for him. You catch them with a big net like butterflies and then put them in a sack."

Finally Nonna falls asleep and I play with a six-sided cube puzzle I know almost by heart. What will I do tomorrow? My mother often brings me stupid toys that I don't know what to do with. I hope tonight Zio Eugenio will fix the balcony drape as he promised he would. I like to look out at the light and especially at the rain. I'd rather look out than go out.

Every afternoon when Giulia has finished putting the kitchen in order, she has to take me out to buy an ice cream so that I can get some fresh air. She doesn't want me in the kitchen but she doesn't mind taking me out in the afternoon, especially because Nonna pays for her ice cream, too. I have to hold her hand because there are a lot of cars in the street and a big crowd of people. Giulia's hand is soft and moist like a sponge, and seems boneless. That's why I say she's like a snail which has come out of its shell. In the street she is terrified that something will happen to me.

Once I saw a color TV. Everything in the street resembles what you see on color TV. If Nonna were to buy one, there'd be no need to take me out. Other than for fresh air.

Nonna has only a black and white TV. As soon as I get back home I turn it on to watch cartoons. One of my cousins comes in and lies quietly on the floor stretched out on his stomach. In her intolerable way, Nonna starts in: "What have you accomplished, Corrado? Have you done your homework? Has Anna got back from the gym? Did Anselmo go to the piano teacher's? Come over here and let me blow your nose! You look so much like poor Ettore. Come, come here next to me...."

It happened exactly as Nonna always said it would. Nonna is dead but it is as if she were not. Zia-Nonna tells the friends who come or telephone to express their condolences that she died of old age. She herself hadn't realized the end was coming but Giulia told her the morning after Nonna's death that Nonna no longer wanted milk for breakfast but only a little coffee and this was definitely a sign. At the table Zia-Nonna hadn't noticed but Giulia also told her that actually Nonna was eating hardly anything at all. In all that confusion at the table nobody could have noticed anyway, except Giulia who found Nonna's plate full when she cleared the table.

Giulia related, too, that on the last mornings when she put the shopping on the table, Nonna said: "Giulia, please, you check the weight of the prosciutto...." Now, says Giulia, Nonna knew very well that she didn't know how to read the new scale, the one with a single pan and the needle with the numbers. Giulia only understands the scale with two pans, the one Pippo broke which had to be replaced, or the old weigh-bridge type which she knew from practice. How could Nonna, if she were in her right mind, have Giulia work a scale that she didn't understand. Giulia told her patiently: "But Signora, you know very well that I can't read this scale!" and Nonna pretended not to have heard and added: "Well, then, is the weight correct?"

The last day, I remember, instead of saying "Let's find the words in the dictionary," Nonna said, "Let's find the *little* words in the dictionary."

This is what Zia-Nonna would have said, not Nonna. Nonna would never have said that. The word "tongue" came up again but Nonna didn't notice. Our game lasted much less than usual.

Now, just as Nonna had predicted, it's my Zia-Nonna who is sitting here. She's asked for a leave of absence from her job and has announced that she'll retire as soon as possible. Otherwise, she said, the household could not go on, everything would go to pieces. And it would cost much more than the difference between her salary and her pension.

Before, Zia-Nonna wore brightly colored clothes and bleached her hair. She's had the hairdresser make her hair gray again and she wears black. No more color on her fingernails or lips.

When Zia-Nonna dies, my mother will have to sit at the table. Then, according to the rule, it would be my turn. But I'm going to leave this house and Naples, too. My only fear is that Nonna may have occupied the whole world. Even the face of the moon, if you see it close up, resembles Nonna.

Unhappily for me, Zia-Nonna doesn't play the word game using Mr. Tommaseo's Dictionary. She tweaks me under the chin instead and always says, "Cutie-pie, cutie-pie!" She spends whole minutes tying bows in my hair. Instead of going out with Giulia, I go out with her in the afternoon. My mother, too, when she was a little girl, went out with the other Nonna who is now dead. Until she got too heavy and her legs gave out.

Translated by Barbara Dow Nucci

THE ELECTRIC TYPEWRITER
by
Francesca Sanvitale

The rainy September cast a low, melancholy, beautiful light. Day after day it caused feelings of detachment and separation, even despair, especially at sunset. For hours Carlo hadn't moved and had passed the idle afternoon without enjoying the September light. His gaze had shifted from the bookshelves, and slowly moved from one object to another. Like one wretched, depraved, or obsessed, he had stared at the orderly piles of newspapers and magazines on little benches and tables, separated according to a personal work method, and gazed at the flowers in the rugs, the elaborately decorated borders. Everything scrutinized in detail but without thought.

He had been trying to pursue, gather, differentiate and thereby destroy a fog behind his eyes that came out to cloud his glasses. This fog had a peculiar characteristic: it dissolved backgrounds and perspectives and outlined things in dusty lights.

For more than a month he had calmed his aggravating restlessness by devoting the entire afternoon to the observation of his studio and he no longer felt the need to go out.

Iris would come back soon and he was waiting for her. His eyes stopped searching the shadows and were cast outside himself, like an object in a surrealistic painting, towards an imagined door. Everything would return to normal in his sight and in the room as soon as Iris turned the key in the lock. As always she would slam the door carelessly and break into his space. She would open a window and lean out, exposing her fat hips, crying out, "Air! Air!" She would observe with disgust the ash tray full of butts. She would hurriedly question him ("How many pages?" "Have you finished?" "How far did you get?").

Out of habit Carlo would not answer. From the kitchen would come the smells of garlic and onion that he found reassuring. The work day was over. In other times, which seemed far away but were not, they would see friends in the evening, go to the theater or a movie.

He had turned sixty-two the day before. Many said he was a great writer, but not too prolific. He had noticed that after sixty almost all writers, for one reason or another, become great writers. The public is lavish with its praise and then forgets all about them.

He gazed at the books, the objects of various size and value, pictures, rugs, arm chairs, divans, and observed that this was what remained of the many words used which formed neither emotions or memories. They had materialized there around him as if he had been the manager of a small, agoraphobic business for forty years.

For him and Iris almost forty years of artistic activity had transformed themselves into a series of objects contained in that middle-class apartment

and in the small seaside apartment. His stories
were born one after the other with relative ease,
and he was convinced that they were always
significant. Iris had said repeatedly in the face of
his uncertainties and anxieties: just write and don't
think about it too much. It's all right, it's all right.
You are an artist. And the future? the future? This had been the
past: an introduction, indeed a necessary introduction. He was sure that the future would be
different in the sense that he finally would grasp
something that he had only vaguely sought inside
himself, he would plunge into the surging depths
that exist below human surfaces. Maybe he would
sell the two apartments. Maybe he would move
abroad. Maybe Iris would die.

Iris kept saying with love or with scorn or with a
particular maternal inflection that he was an eternal
child. This was the way she forced him in bed to
touch the depths of his weakness, and at the
moment he understood it she would brush it away
with a slight-of-hand. In a kind of dream, a show
ad absurdum, he found himself practicing a virility
without tenderness, only frenzy, and in that kind of
game or dream he was the tyrant and she the slave.

Iris was very fat and had become old. She didn't
care. She seemed to believe that their nights would
never change. She had assumed the role of trainer
and in the morning Carlo was ready for the ring of
his studio, at the desk, strictly tied to her and to
that room, unfit for life or any other kind of woman.
He still desired Iris because she allowed him the
vices his mind needed. Iris barred any novelty, she
obliterated defeats. She prevented a calm reflection on the meaning of existence, but she also

prevented thought from sinking into darkness,
beyond the curtain of flowing images.

For a month his depression had deepened and his
headaches, anxiety, and tiredness had increased.
He was forced to withdraw into himself. The
doctor and Iris consulted behind his back. He had
come to a passage, perhaps providential: he had to
reflect, to understand something that had escaped
him. Then he could go on.

He was not writing anymore. That didn't matter.
He was too tired, trapped in a dismal listlessness.
His face played annoying tricks, but the doctor said
the symptoms were entirely gratuitous and
connected with his nerves. The same with the
nausea that every once in a while rose from his guts
for no reason. He had to let himself rest.

He went out on the balcony and looked to the
left toward the neighboring balcony. Almost dark.
The other window was illuminated. He heard the
regular, muffled noise of the electric typewriter.
Short pauses, followed by a clicking. He sat down,
even though the cool wind bothered him. He
watched the wind shaking the stems of the long,
thin, nearly wilted carnations that Orlando, the next
door neighbor, didn't take care of. They drooped
over the railing in small dry clusters.

He was aware of the traffic on the street. He
listened to the stopping and starting of the electric
typewriter. With an idiotic joy every day he tried
to imagine what in the world Orlando was writing.
It might be a new novel. He had already written
two of them, very much like two stories, and not
much longer. Competent representations. Pleasant
female characters. Plausible dialogue. The stories

that Orlando told were easy to understand. Orlando himself was more difficult to understand.

Since he had to rest, Carlo often amused himself by inventing stories to the rhythm of the electric typewriter. He was free to tell himself nonsensical stories, imitating the avant-garde buried before his youth. He drew out and put together odd bunches of images in the surrealistic manner, or composed obscene love songs, or sonnets in the manner of Carducci. It was his solitary and entirely new way to play in the dark silence and also to feel that his mind, like an enclosed reservoir, was full of words that mingled in amazing fantasies even without his willing them. He seemed to have regained a sense of freedom, a taste of childhood, of adolescence.

From Orlando's apartment came a longer caesura than usual. Immediately Carlo imagined in the darkness before him the gigantic ectoplasm of a hand suspended over the keyboard and he waited. He thought only one exact phrase: maybe that clicking will never start up again.

In that case, in such an extraordinary and unprecedented case, the silence would become high, magnificent, charged with emotion. Orlando and he, like two astronauts detached from their spaceship would move away into empty space grasping each other tightly, quickly disappearing, exactly alike and mute. But the clicking recommenced and Carlo heard within it the arrogant superiority of youth.

Orlando lived alone. He wrote articles for a newspaper and was a researcher at the university. A girl named Gina visited him at irregular intervals and lived with him for two or three days. Carlo had never understood their real relationship. One could suppose it a stability that had lasted for years. Or a complete casualness that had kept them apart as it had united them. He spied on them. They kept a rhythmical pace on the street as they walked in step. They dressed alike, faded jeans and nice sweaters, colored shirts, jackets. They gave the impression of cautious confidence and harmony. They had the habit of stopping every once in awhile as they walked and looking into each other's eyes with a slight smile. Gina would toss back her long straight hair with a loose, careless motion, and bending her head would gather it in one hand, bringing it forward over her shoulders.

Carlo watched them as if they were two people to be robbed. Their affectations as a couple, their over-harmonious movements made him feel spiteful. He criticized them: according to him they were showing off on a stage and Orlando would have to watch out because that was not life.

In a certain sense he desired both of them. He allowed himself sexual fantasies or extravagant erotic impulses because he knew he was depressed and wanted to amuse himself. Orlando was thirty, slender as a fifteen-year-old but without the aggressiveness. He went through the world taking his pleasures with a casual elegance and a secret obstinacy. Carlo envied him with an intensity and confusion so strong that at times it seemed like love.

The doorbell rang. Carlo shuffled down the hall and opened the door.

"Excuse me for bothering you. Can you lend me your Collins?"

Orlando spoke with a pleasant urbanity.

Carlo made a brusk gesture, turned on the lights, preceded him into the studio. Orlando's self-assurance was stupid. Why on earth did he have to have that particular dictionary? He bent over with difficulty and his head spun. A whirl, a dangerous dizziness, passed through his brain. "Here is the Collins," he said, panting a little. "I have it by chance." He was observing Orlando's body: his well-built arms with long muscles, his chest and slender hips. He possessed a supple gracefulness, a suggestion of boyishness with his sudden gestures. His eyes were slightly convex, clear and very still, like those of certain insects.

Orlando looked around, a little unsure of himself. "I see," he remarked, in a tone of respect by no means humble, "that you have the Tommaseo Bellini dictionary in the first edition of eight volumes!" He made a slight gesture toward the volumes.

Carlo said nothing. There was a pause. Orlando began to say that he would be leaving for New York the next day. "On a scholarship for one year. I wanted to say good-bye because I'm leaving my apartment. I'm sorry I didn't see more of you." He stopped. He frowned and added, "Naturally it was unavoidable. It's hard for anyone who writes in the province...."

Carlo gave him an uncomprehending look and interrupted him: "The province? What has the province to do with it?"

"I meant Italy. The games they play everywhere...."

He smiled.

Silence reigned. Carlo straightened some newspapers. "One can write anywhere," he mumbled.

He was about to add something else but Orlando was heading rapidly toward the front door. "I'll bring it back right away," he said in a high voice. Shrill, a sort of warble.

Carlo was alone again. He turned off the lights. Over Orlando's bed was an Escher poster. In the living room a few pieces of light wood furniture, red and black director's chairs. Basically the boy was almost poor and, compared to him, lived like an ascetic. He didn't own a house and earned little. He owned only an electric typewriter. But Orlando made him angry: he didn't realize the complexity of the problem, he didn't even understand that he was dealing more with an enigma than a profession. Or both? At this point he became angry with himself also. That happened to someone suffering from nerves: small exterior events, little upsets resulted in inner disturbances. Orlando was going to New York and consequently Carlo wouldn't be able to know what turn that life had taken. This bothered him, annoyed him very much. In six months of being close neighbors they had talked only foolishness, letting the two women take the lead in their rare encounters. Did he like Conrad? Did he like James? Had he read, for instance, *Kiss of the Spider Woman*? What was the plot of the novel he was writing? and *his* novels? what did he *really* think of them?

He didn't hear the clicking any more. A particular silence fell over the house and over him.

The lock turned and in a moment Iris was in the studio.

"Well," she said at once. Her voice left no doubt of her invasion. "Still in the dark?" She turned on the light and began taking in everything with her inspection. "Nasty weather outside. It seems like winter. Better to stay in the house." She threw a newspaper on the desk. "The interview came out. The photograph of you doesn't look bad. If I were a young reader it would give me wicked thoughts." She giggled. She took the ashtray.

"What is there to eat?" Carlo asked.

"Nothing, why?" She broke into one of her typical laughs. It would be a special dish, then. She went into the hall exclaiming, "I can't wait to take off my shoes!"

For a moment he thought of following her, of taking her by the shoulders, of making love quickly, before supper, as they used to do when they were young. He sat down and lowered his head in his hands. Again the doorbell as he tried to rouse himself from his torpor. Orlando was already back with the dictionary and was looking at him quizzically. "Aren't you feeling well?" He stepped forward to hold him up or give him support, but Carlo shook his head, overcome by anger and drowsiness. "Certainly not," he managed to say in a kind of whisper. "Nothing is wrong, nothing, do you understand?"

Orlando moved back to reestablish the space he had violated.

"Just remember!" Carlo believed he was shouting, "just remember that you don't kid around with words!" But he only thought he was shouting and he had lost the thought again. That wasn't what he wanted to throw in Orlando's face to waken him from his conventional faith.

The only words that came to his mind were even more senseless: have you read Tolstoy? Have you read Stendhal? and Dickens? and De Quincey? and

Dickinson? and Chekhov? and Goethe? and Dostoevski? and....

He was forming a kind of litany in his head that numbed him as though he were counting sheep to go to sleep. He closed his eyes.

Orlando stood there stock still, in amazement, looking at him. He barely murmured, "I wanted to say good-bye, excuse me." Nothing happened. Carlo's heavy body folded over in a slow-motion faint and his eyelids opened and closed as if he had swallowed poison. His eyes were rolling wildly.

Orlando backed away in little steps. "Signora Iris," he murmured again. "I don't think Signor Carlo feels very well."

Iris came out unconcerned and shook her head. "It's nerves, depression," she said.

"I'm so sorry," whispered Orlando. "I'm sure he'll feel better soon. Please give him my best wishes."

Carlo heard Iris and Orlando talking and saying good-bye. He heard him go out. He heard the noises that punctuated his afternoons: the turn of the lock, the click of light. He felt that he was sinking into a deep hell: perhaps it was really the well he had dreamed up, the darkness that leads to consciousness, to the horror that right words come from. He had avoided it all his life and he wasn't sure he wanted this ordeal. "Iris," he shouted, "Iris! Iris!"

A menacing silence fell. The shadow assailed him, forced pain on him. What was this empty room of knowledge that, like a twin to torture, his nightmare symbolized? He thought confusedly of Orpheus, of Pamino, of efforts, of hard labors described in fables and was about to grasp the

meaning of what he was seeking, as if it were
something struggling to enter his heart with simple
clarity. Perhaps they were the true words, the
unforgettable stories. "Iris!" he shouted again. He
stood up staggering, nerve-racked and shaken by so
much emotion. Suddenly he vomited.

The doorbell rang for the third time. Iris ran to
the door and opened it.

"How is he today?" the doctor said as he
entered.

Iris dried a tear with the palm of her hand. "He
seems worse to me." She spoke softly to keep
Carlo from hearing. "Much worse. But he doesn't
realize...he has never realized anything...."

The doctor clapped her on the back. "Cheer up,
Signora," he said good-naturedly. "Let's go and
have a look at him."

Translated by Martha King

PINK
by
Monica Sarsini

Pale, gentle, effeminate, sweet-smelling, blushing delicateness. The sunsets on the highway from Rome to Florence with black mountains standing out against a limpid summer sky. Women with their gray hair in a bun, crocheting as they linger in bed, while the house moves along to the pace of the housekeeper's steps, not over-concerned with time. Sled-riding downhill over the snow, or going down the slides in the melancholy city-parks, muddled by an aimless confusion of colored balloons. Pigs, spring fruit blossoms, tongue and gums, tonalities of the ear. Heat, warmth, sugar-coated almonds. Apologetic attempts, an oasis, a limbo that falls apart as everything around it closes in. Flamingos, abundance of bourgeois objects, gaudy, affected, wanting to appear lovely, but not even decently passable. Nausea, cotton fluff, fear of solitude, of growing up in silence without accomplices. Unnatural nature, spectacular Epiphanies. To abstain from declaration, to fear judgment, to refrain from argument, to be tired of fighting; to wish to go back and stay innocent. Arms akimbo, listening to the confessions of someone half-reclining, elbow resting on the bed-table, legs all hugged up tight. Bits of Carnival-time, lotions, hair drawn at the back of the neck, making peace, having no one to wait for. Family ideology, some fish, hard candy. Antique but not old laces, cobwebs, soap. Pink with black, pink with orange. Illusions, hopes, mirages, unkept promises, when one wishes to believe that the enthusiasm with which we embrace a cause is genuine. Dazzling angel faces in the clouds, Pontormo-pink, rose-pink. Going on singing when the others in the choir have stopped. A promising future. Habit, unpretentious desire. Black people's palms. Kindergarten girls' collar bows, ribbons on doors and in shop windows when a baby girl's birth is not to be kept a secret. Ostrich feathers, clouds, vapors, fumes, nebulous billows evaporating against the metallic gray of the city. Cactus flowers, dog teats, tender skin in the midst of aged pachydermic roughness. Color without substance, color that does not take wing, does not become a vegetable, does not reach maturity. Rosolio rose liqueur.

LAVENDER

With leftovers from dawn, lavender drew together in a faint light and, from the pavement, gazed on the familiar indifference of places still uninhabited by the devourers of time. Lighting a cigarette, its long tender legs nonchalantly strolled into a puddle and waited there, in that vague position, for the corner cafe to open. It kept disappearing and reappearing, gently vanishing, like someone trying to come into the world although already there – knowing it would not have a voice, but hoping for a sudden joy, like the surprise at a party, long put off because of shyness.

It was up early; the city streets were deserted. At the newspaper stall, the bored vendor waited, looking out from the wall of magazines, for the daily newspapers to arrive by bicycle.

Lavender saw the daylight, the swift dissipation of people addicted to rushing even though no one is chasing them. Habitually lazy, it tried to feign an air of initiative which quickly faded away because it had no memory for how things should be imitated. It changed its mind again, still keeping that ambiguous peace which comes from knowing we're not observed. Stumbling among the motor-bikes that leave a wound in the asphalt as they brake, it slipped into the cafe, to take shape again over the tablecloths covering the newly-dusted tables, and along the glass-divider that keeps the dust off the spongy muffins and crisp cookies.

It lingered there for a long while in a sort of doze, resigned to the wait, indifferent to its haphazard mood, and then went on to idle, void of purpose, over faces that must be re-composed after the secret battle of night, so that no trace of a powerful dream may remain on the vanquished cheeks and burnt-out gaze. It searches for itself in a shop window, surprised to meet itself. Silence intertwines with its fingers like a long thread that is hard to unravel. The fear of death returns, and this feeling dissolves all consciousness of necessity. Its understanding of death is a dispassionate awareness that cannot be shaken off.

The color hovered about and arrived later, within touching distance of the words that were yet to be said.

SILVER

To seek each other, reflect each other everywhere, aglow in the darkness. To get to know objects, to remember where we are, to shine out, catching light, playing with reflections. To soothe, marvel, transmit an exquisite fairy-tale aura to an image, add movement to a glance, prolong a look, become enchanted with superficiality. To be surprised and stupefied, to recall magical associations, suggestive impressions, to slip away from time. To stop and try to see more than what is there, to throw doubt on what we actually see. To exalt luminosity and the essence of angles. To decorate, celebrate, ornament, make things memorable. To wait no longer for day-time to have something of night, for night to be space. To be assured of an opening, a point of escape, a gap in material life that we may pass through, like music. The feeling of cool relief, haste, even disloyalty. Haziness, a mixing of fire and oceans. To do away with surfaces in order to avoid depth. A flight from the impulse to perpetuate.

GREEN

Never still. It breathes, ripples, becomes part of the air, swelling, rocking, trembling. It races, jumps or sneaks about. Deaf, mute, unwary of adversaries, translucent, it has no beginning, no end. Its profundity reaches every niche of the forest, swinging with the trees, shaping the wind. Weaving in and out, it creates mazes in space and a soft musky odor over the cottony oceanic silence. It is a sign of life among the plants and of seduction for reptiles; it is comforting, cordial, digestive. In shades of various intensity, penetrated by sounds, a rush of freshness that is unripe, flexible, an exceptional dancer not afraid of the world it owns, the energizer of metallic light, opposed to vainglory. It mirrors nothing, neither the tree next to the house nor the lizard on the garden wall. Meadows, pastures, prairies, plum trees, pine trees, parks, pistachios. It moves forever ahead, but never escapes, letting others search for it, mobile and spectacular. Verdi, the national anthem, Maurizio Nannucci, vegetables, Verdiglione. Fertile, frankly sexual, it laughs gurgling, greets you with a wide grin, with open arms, with the firm stance of a mountain climber or a gymnastics teacher. A painstaking seamstress, an expert at embroidering hems and borders, sewing buttonholes. Apparently unacquainted with nostalgia or bitterness, loved by everyone. "Why is green suffocated by black whereas white isn't?" Because it exists outside of itself, always the host. Greenbacks, being in the hills. It has a task to perform, a mission to accomplish, never thinking over past choices, destined for immortality. Long greenish distances are liberated at every passing. Alert and aware, it is young, and although others may try hard not to die or go insane, not wanting to remain in this world, but lacking the courage to leave it, green is contented, fulfilling its duty, aspiring to maturity. Like a person without dreams who laughs and smiles, not too concerned with itself, eating what comes along, out of curiosity for new tastes, uncomplaining, nonchalantly swallowing tranquillizers, closing its eyes when its head aches, calmly dozing at the theater, unmoved by boredom.

WHITE

Disintegrated voices, where all sounds fade away, calls reach their end, and space absorbs them; where words go when they sink to the deep or get thrown ashore. Can anyone express thought without the voice inevitably taking on those characteristics, imposing authority through acceptance of prohibitions, seductions, gestures, and the mazes of propositions that sadden words, forcing infinite repetition like someone who tries desperately to sit down, get up and go away. These are people who talk to each other, seek each other and adopt a pose when they meet. People who are forever late so that they may act as though they had never come, while others cannot remain where their desires lead them because they are afraid to die. Lines of shade, light, pointed angles, openings, ravines, short runs, dense steam and then periods of thin silence. Hands clasping the knees like cradles or hats, warm lips pressed tight that focus ahead. Corners in which waiting is immersed, over the knotty tree branches. A relaxed oval face that crosses hazily above, below and through another face, momentarily as in a port. A glitter of pleasure while glancing about, finally at rest and out of the wind. No need for experience in these seas. At the wedding tomorrow, it will be catapulted among white lilies, rice and sheets. White eyes and teeth stuck in a dark face, with luminously incandescent pearls at the ear-lobes. The fingernails standing out against the tan skin are like shells on the cliffs, whereas the white curves of the nails seem to be ephemeral shields protecting a desire to streak a furrow in the earth. The nails are open shells that embrace in the warmth of the skin. It is the dawn breaking from night's embrace while, on the terrace rail, shreds of curdled spiderwebs swing from the green columns, hanging by a slender thread. The railing has blossomed ephemerous white growths that sway in the wind like sleepwalkers. The baker has set the baskets of warm bread all in a row next to the door, while way beyond, the thoughts of life spread ever wider on the horizon, arching softly, making the end imperceptible, slipping away, never stumbling, like a laugh that spreads, a voice reaching the bed, breath, a high floor, a white ceiling. The distant white whale among the icebergs. The white cliffs of Dover, Siamese cats, polar bears and ghosts, choir-boys, the uniforms of nurses, cooks and sailors. White telephones. Aniseed, milk, fresh almond and walnut kernels, bananas. Salt. Sails over the waves and a white band holding back dark hair. Pelican swans, a bone in a dog's mouth, elephant tusks. Lambs, marble quarries, the moon behind the clouds, dazzling blades, Snow White, snow, canvas for painting, sleepless 'white-mares.' Space suits, zebra stripes on the asphalt, zebras in the savanna, white chessmen and checkers. A starched tuxedo shirt, egg white, cigarette paper.

Thin crests of foam that break against the ship's side.

Translated by Gloria Italiano

AUTHORS

ANNA BANTI (1895-1985) lived in Florence where for many years she directed the art-literary journal *Paragone* founded by her husband Roberto Longhi. Her novels and short stories have a historical setting, but with a modern message. They are imaginatively focused on such historical figures as the painter Artemisia and the French wife of the last Medici Grand Duke of Tuscany, Marguerite-Louise. Her story here deals with a nineteenth-century family that is contaminated at the core by the hatred of husband-father-breadwinner and wife-mother-housewife. A "typical" family situation, except that in this case the woman finds courage to resist, if only passively.

GRAZIA DELEDDA (1871-1936) was born and lived in Nuoro, Sardinia until she married and moved to Rome in 1900. Her novels and short stories, set in an archaic yet changing Sardinia, received early acclaim. Deledda won the Nobel Prize for Literature in 1926. She wrote nearly forty novels and collections of short stories in as many years. The first English translation of her autobiographical novel, *Cosima,* translated by Martha King, has been published by Italica Press.

PAOLA DRIGO (1876-1938) was born in Castelfranco in the Veneto and died in Padua. Her three collections of stories and one novel, *Maria Zef* (published in 1936 and reissued in 1982), deal with the problems of the rural north. She is acclaimed for her realistic portrayals of aristocrats, farm owners and workers in a changing agricultural society. A movie version of *Maria Zef* was made in 1954, and in 1981 it was produced for TV. Blossom S. Kirschenbaum's translation of the complete novel has just been published by the University of Nebraska Press.

Authors

NATALIA GINZBURG, born in 1916, is perhaps best-known to English readers through the translation of many of her books. Her simple, conversational style in such works as *Voices in the Evening, Family Sayings,* and *The Little Virtues* has won her a wide readership in the United States and England as well as in Italy. She works as an editor for Einaudi publishing house and also serves as a member in the Italian Parliament.

GEDA JACOLUTTI (1921-1989) was born in Udine, where she taught in a women's public school for more than thirty years. In addition to short stories she wrote poetry and had five books of her translations from the classics published in Italy. Jacolutti directed a graphics and poetry series, *Pagine Provinciali,* for the publisher La Nuova Base di Udine. This publishing house also brought out collections of her short stories: *Gli itinerari* (1978), *Singolare Femminile* (1983), and *Il passo degli angeli* (1984).

GINA LAGORIO was born in Piedmont, in north-west Italy and at present lives and works in Milan. She has produced novels, essays and plays. In 1983 she was awarded the Premio Flaiano for the theater for her comedy *Raccontami quella di Flic.* The novel *Tosca dei gatti* (Premio Viareggio 1984) was first issued in 1983. She is known for her portrayal of "new" women who have forged nontraditional lifestyles.

ROSETTA LOY's prize-winning novel, *La strade di polvere,* a fictional history set in the politically turbulent nineteenth century, was on the list of best-selling books in Italy for many weeks. She was born in Rome of a Roman mother and a father from Piedmont (the locale of her recent novel). Loy has published four novels and a book of short stories since 1974.

DACIA MARAINI has published novels, short stories, plays and poetry for more than 20 years. In 1962, when she was 26, her first novel, *La vacanza,* appeared with a rather equivocal preface written by Alberto Moravia. This novel was surprisingly successful and four printings immediately followed. Marini's next novel, *L'età del malessere,* won the international award Formentor, which caused much controversy – how could such a young (and pretty) woman also be a good writer? Dacia Marini's protagonists, always women, are often outsiders looking in on the "good life." They are sometimes the victims of deliberate male repression, but more often they are simply playing out a bleak twentieth-century drama in which they have little or no control. Maraini, who presently lives in Rome, is considered one of the most influential writers associated with the feminist movement in Italy, and her fiction and poetry reflect her political concerns.

MILENA MILANI, like Monica Sarsini, is an artist as well as a writer, having had over forty one-person shows since 1965. Many of her collections of short stories, poetry, and her novels have won national prizes. She was born in Savona but has lived in Rome since childhood. Her short fiction has also appeared in various Italian newspapers.

MARINA MIZZAU teaches psychology at the University of Bologna. She writes about daily, apparently insignificant, incidents, such as a trip on an elevator or crossing the street, that nevertheless have wider implications. The conflicts, confusion, embarrassment of her characters put aspects of the human psyche in high relief. Her publications include *Tecniche narrative e romanzo contemporaneo* (Mursia, 1965), *Prospettive della comunicazione interpersonale* (Il Mulino, 1974), *Eco e Narciso: Parole e silenze nel confitto uomo-donna* (Boringhieri, 1979) and *L'ironia* (Feltrinelli, 1984).

GIULIANA MORANDINI lives in Rome where she works in the field of literary and drama criticism with special reference to German culture. Her works include *E allora mi hanno rinchiusa* (Premio Viareggio, 1977), an inquiry into mental homes for women; *I cristalli di Vienna* (translated as *Bloodstains* by Blossom S. Kirschenbaum, St. Paul, MN: New Rivers Press, 1987), the novel in which her family and wartime memories mirror the crisis of reason and culture; *La voce che è in lei* (1980) on the works of nineteenth-century women writers; *Caffè Specchi* (Premio Viareggio, 1983), the intense story of a woman in timeless Trieste. Her interest in Central European heritage and psychoanalysis also affects her children's works (*Ricerca Carlotta,* 1979). She edited the German edition of Pier Paolo Pasolini's plays (Frankfurt,

1984). Her most recent work is the novel *Angelo à Berlino* (1987), which portrays the traditions and conflicts of Berlin, intermingled with personal recollections.

ELSA MORANTE (1912-1985) is considered by many to be one of the best Italian writers of this century. Though she wrote few books, they have proved durable, outside any current writing fashion. *La storia* (1947) was a best-seller for many weeks and was made into a television film in 1987. She also wrote *L'isola di Arturo,* the story of young Arthur's growing up on the island of Procida, from innocence to knowledge of the corrupt world. Her last novel was *Aracoeli.* Perhaps because of the books' popularity, Italian critics have been divided in their appraisal of them.

MARIA OCCHIPINTI was arrested in Ragusa, Sicily, as an activist opposing compulsory conscription in January 1945 when she was 24 years old. She was first exiled to the island of Ustica and later incarcerated in Palermo. "The Benedictines," recalling these events, is from her autobiographical novel, *Una donna di Ragusa* (Milan: Luciano Landi, 1957; Feltrinelli, 1976). Now in her sixties, Occhipinti lives in Rome with her daughter after living many years in England, Switzerland and the United States where she worked in hospitals, private homes and as a fur tailor. After returning to Italy, she resumed her political advocacy for victims of persecution, speaking out in defense of the Sicilian farmers against state expropriations and against nuclear weapons. In 1975 *Una donna di Ragusa* won the Zafferana Etna Prize, and in 1988 it was awarded the Cesare Pavese Prize.

ANNA MARIA ORTESE was born in Rome in 1914 and was twenty-three when her first book, *Angelici dolori,* came out in 1937. In 1950 her second novel was published, *L'infanta sepolta,* and three years later the successful collection of short stories, *Il mare non bagna Napoli,* which was awarded the Premio Viareggio. Many other prize-winning novels followed. Ortese has also contributed cultural articles to Italian newspapers. She now lives a reclusive life in Rapallo and continues to publish her visionary works in realistic settings. A complete collection of her short stories in English translation is forthcoming from McPherson & Co.

FABRIZIA RAMONDINO, born in Naples in 1936, has lived in Spain, France and Germany. In 1960 she returned to Naples to live, contributing to the newspaper *Il Mattino*. Among her publications are *Napoli, i disoccupati organizzati: I Protagonisti raccontano* (1977), *Althenopis* (1981), *Storie di Patio* (1983), *Taccuino Tedesco* (1987), and *Un Giorno e mezzo* (1988), a novel about life in Naples in the late 1960s.

FRANCESCA SANVITALE was born in Milan; studying and working in Florence until the sixties, she then moved to Rome where she now lives. She has published three novels and numerous essays on contemporary fiction. For many years she has written for newspapers, magazines and television. Her acute psychological observations make her novels and short stories rewarding reading; an especially poignant novel explores a mother-daughter relationship, *Madre e figlia* (1980). Because she has known different regions of Italy so well her settings can just as easily be Milan, Florence or Rome.

MONICA SARSINI is a thirty-five year old Florentine multimedia artist. Her colorful paper collages have been exhibited in galleries in the principle cities of Italy. Her publications include *Crepacuore* and *Crepapelle*, both by Vanni Scheiwiller of Milan, and a novella "Lapo" appearing in the October 1988 issue of the literary review *Linea d'Ombra*. Her collages have also been printed in three limited editions, with numbered copies, by the Exit art publishing house. The five colors presented here are taken from *Colorare* (Bologna, 1984).

TRANSLATORS

HELEN BAROLINI lives in Scarborough, New York. Her stories, translations, reviews, essays and poetry have appeared in *Kenyon Review, Paris Review, New York Review of Books, Antioch Review,* and elsewhere. For her work, she has won an American Book Award from the Before Columbus Foundation and a creative writing grant from the National Endowment for the Arts. She has translated many books from Italian into English; she originated and compiled *The Dream Book: An Anthology of Writings by Italian American Women.* She has published the novels, *Umbertina* and *Love in the Middle Ages.* Her most recent book is *Festa: Recipes and Recollections of Italy* (New York: Harcourt, Brace, Jovanovich, 1988).

DICK DAVIS is a British free-lance writer, poet, critic, and translator. He has translated *The Little Virtues* (New York: Seaver Books, 1986) and *The City and the House* (New York: Seaver Books, 1987) by Natalia Ginzburg into English

GLORIA ITALIANO received an M.A. in Italian Literature from the University of Wisconsin and an M.S. in Linguistics from Georgetown University in Washington, DC. Presently Associate Professor of English Language at the University of Florence, Italy, she previously taught simultaneous and consecutive translations at the School for Interpreters in Florence. Her translations include *St. Teresa of Avila* by Giorgio Papasogli (New York: Society of St. Paul, 1964), *Pescia nel Rinascimento: All'Ombra di Firenze,* by Judith C. Brown, *In the Shadow of Florence* (Oxford: Oxford University Press, 1982), and *An English Prince: Newcastle's Machiavellian Political Guide to Charles II* (Pisa: Giardini Editors, 1988). *Four English/Italian Stories - Experiments in Translation* (Lake Bluff, IL: Jupiter Press, 1983) reflects her academic interests in socio-linguistic theory, language transfer, and their applications to foreign-language teaching.

Translators

MARTHA KING received her Ph.D. in Italian from the University of Wisconsin. Her translations and articles on Italian literature have been published in *Modern Language Notes, James Joyce Quarterly, Italian Quarterly, Translation, Stories, The Literary Review* and other journals. The National Endowment for the Arts awarded her a translation grant in 1980-81. In 1988 Italica Press published her translations of *Cosima* by Grazia Deledda and *Family Chronicle* by Vasco Pratolini. Her interest has long focused on Sardinian writers, particularly Deledda, whose biography she is presently writing. She has lived in Tuscany since 1979.

BLOSSOM S. KIRSCHENBAUM works in Comparative Literature at Brown University. She has published articles in *Sage* and *MELUS* and translated Giuliana Morandini's *I cristalli di Vienna* as *Bloodstains* (St. Paul, MN: New Rivers Press, 1987) and *Fables from Trastevere* (1976), the verse of Trilussa. Her translation of *Maria Zef* has recently been published by the University of Nebraska Press.

HENRY MARTIN has lived and worked in Italy since 1965. After receiving his B.A. from Bowdoin College and his M.A. from New York University in English literature, he taught English language and literature for several years at Università Bocconi in Milan. He works now as a freelance art critic and translator. His translation of *The Iguana* by Anna Maria Ortese was published in 1987 (Kingston, NY: McPherson & Company), and he was recently rewarded a National Endowment of the Arts grant to translate thirty of Ortese's short stories. His translation of Giorgio Manganelli's *Tutti gli errori (All the Errors)* will appear with McPherson & Co. early in 1990.

BARBARA DOW NUCCI graduated from Mt. Holyoke College in 1965 and completed her M.Ed. at Boston University in 1973. Originally from Maine, she has lived and worked in Naples, Italy, for more than twenty years. She teaches Italian and Italian contemporary society to American students. Her other interests include international education and comparative women's studies, in addition to translating the work of Italian women writers.

MARGHERITA PIVA was born and lives in Udine where she teaches English and English literature in a scientific high school. She graduated in 1972 from Università di Udine with a thesis on "Folklore Figures in Robert Herrick's Works," and has continued her research of folklore in early seventeenth-century English minor poetry, including two years at Reading University. She returned to Italy to teach and continue her literary and folklore studies, with special emphasis on analogies between Italian and British Celtic folklore. Her articles include "William Browne, Marino, France, and the Third Book of Britannia's Pastorals" in collaboration with Prof. Cedric Brown of Reading University; "Gnomi e folletti in Friuli e nelle Isole Britanniche," "Folklore e Romance in *A Midsummer Night's Dream,*" and "Mannerismo e Miniatura in *Nimphidia* di Michael Drayton."

WILLIAM WEAVER is well-known for his translations of such Italian writers as Alberto Moravia, Italo Calvino, Umberto Eco *(The Name of the Rose, Foucault's Pendulum)* and many others. He is also the author of books about Giuseppe Verdi and Eleanora Duse. Weaver's articles about Italy appear in *The New York Times, The Financial Times* and numerous other publications. He lives in the Tuscan hills near Monte San Savino.

GLOSSARY

Basso: in Naples, a ground-floor room of an old apartment building opening right onto the street and sometimes inhabited by an entire family.

Callas: Maria Callas.

Excelsior: A deluxe hotel and bathing beach located at Venezia Lido.

Gattó: Neapolitan potato pie.

Nannucci, Maurizio: A conceptual artist who has supposedly photographed every shade of green leaf in existence.

Neapolitan mastiff: a very large dog with great folds of excess skin and known for its intimidating appearance and pleasant disposition.

Nola's Feastday: the annual ceremony of the Dance of the Lilies at Nola, twenty miles south of Naples. The tradition began sixteen centuries ago when the townspeople greeted the return from exile of their bishop, Paulinus, with bunches of lilies. Trade guild competition led eventually to the use of long poles to carry the lilies, then to the huge wooden steeples of today, fifty feet or higher, borne by teams of fifty men.

Nonna: Italian for grandmother, granny, grandma, nana.

Real: an old Spanish silver coin.

Scudo: a large silver coin used in Italy until the end of World War II.

Totó: Stage name of Antonio De Curtis (1898-1967), Neapolitan comic film actor most popular for his film characterization of an unsmiling but sympathetic bourgeois figure, likened by international film critics to Buster Keaton.

Verdi: A play on the word *verde* meaning "green" and the composer name Giuseppe Verdi.

Verdiglione: A famous Italian psychoanalyst whose name carries associations of green and is rhythmically right.

Visconti: Luchino Visconti, the film-maker.

Zia; Zio, Ziu: literally "aunt" and "uncle" but sometimes used as complimentary titles for older people.

203

*This Book Was Completed on August 1, 1989 at
Italica Press, New York, New York and Was
Set in Galliard. It Was Printed on 50 lb
Glatfelter Natural Paper with
a Smyth-Sewn Binding by
McNaughton & Gunn,
Ann Arbor, MI
U. S. A.*
*   *
*